PRAISE FOR DARRELL PITT

'I found myself laughing out loud which rarely happens.'
Sondra Kerby

'An amazing book that has all the elements
of a great whodunnit.'
Ursula Sorensen

'I'm very much looking forward to reading the next book in
the series.'
Alice Hazelbaker

'This was a fun book to read. It had me laughing
a lot throughout.'
Sandy Mill

' I look forward to future installments.'
Caley Gredig

'What an awesome book!'
Michelle

BY DARRELL PITT

The Boy from Earth
Balloon Girls
A Toaster on Mars

Teen Superheroes
Book I: Diary of a Teenage Superhero
Book II: The Doomsday Device
Book III: The Battle for Earth
Book IV: The Twisted Future
Book V: Terminal Fear
Book VI: The Invisible Weapon
Book VII: The Alpha Project

Teen Superhero Bounty Hunters
Book I: Snakebite
Book II: Fear Fight
Book III: Stormfront
Book IV: Past Shadows
Book V: One Small Step

The Steampunk Detective Adventures
Book I: The Firebird Mystery
Book II: The Secret Abyss
Book III: The Broken Sun
Book IV: The Monster Within
Book V: The Lost Sword

Rosie Ryan Cozy Mysteries
Book I: Sun, Surf and Murder
Book II: Rings, Rocks and Murder
Book III: Knives, Knots and Murder
Book IV: Flowers, Fish and Murder
Book V: Pizza, Pugs and Murder
Book VI: Aliens, Apples and Murder
Book VII: Cats, Castles and Murder

DARRELL PITT

Knives, Knots and Murder

A ROSIE RYAN COZY MYSTERY

BOOK THREE

KENT STREET PRESS

kentstreetpress.com

This edition published by Kent Street Press, 2025

ISBN: 978-1-923360-41-9 (paperback)

ISBN: 978-1-923360-32-7 (ebook)

A catalogue record of this book is available from the National Library of Australia.

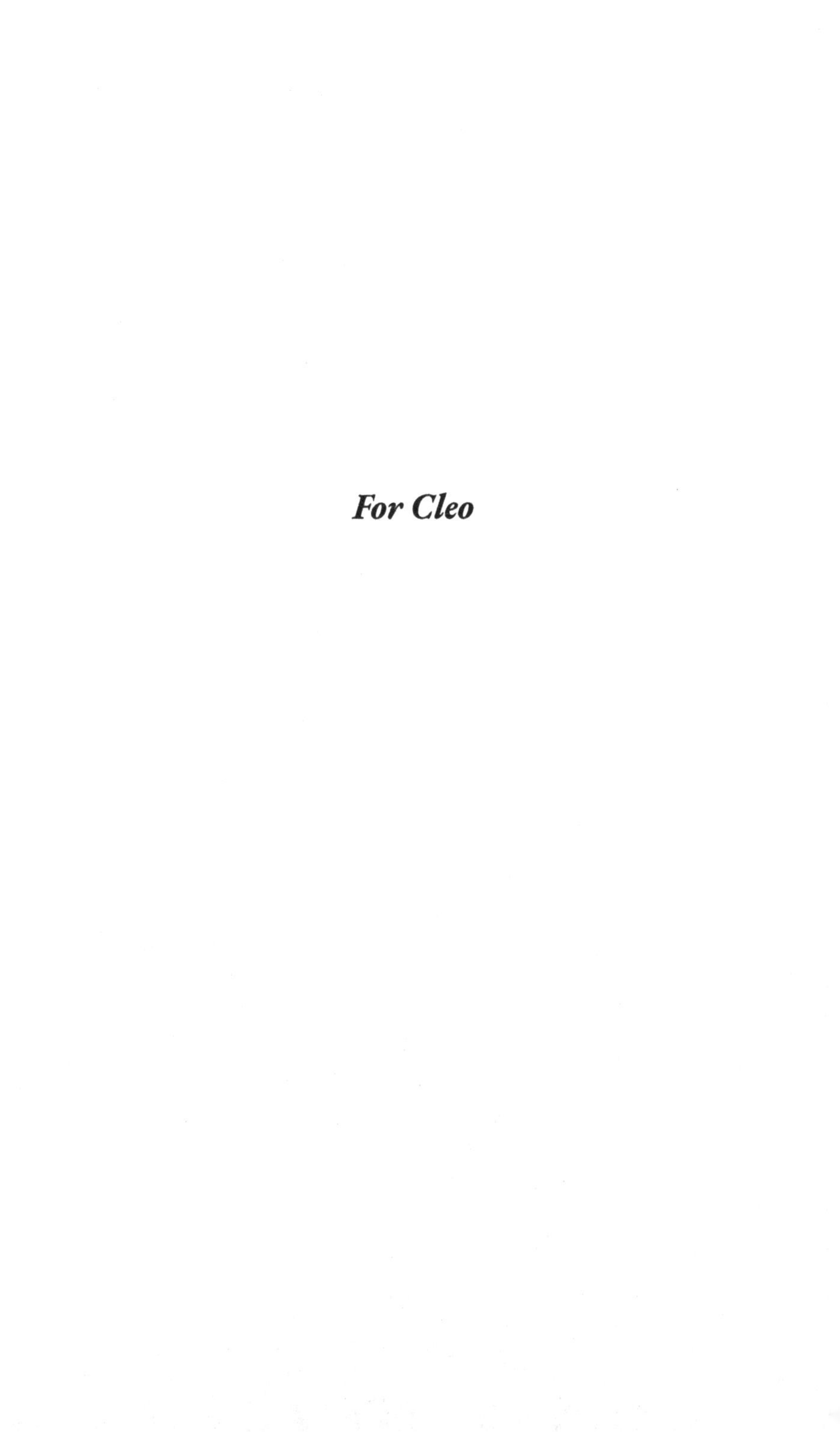

For Cleo

1

'That is the most preposterous explanation I have ever heard,' Wanda Gibson declared loudly.

This proclamation was met with silence by the Cape Carson Mystery Book Club members. Wanda Gibson was a big bulldog of a woman with a wonderful brain, but terrible manners. Most—although not all—of the other club members tolerated Wanda because of her intelligence. One person who fell into the *not all* category was Marlene Hogan, a large woman with round fire engine red framed glasses. She usually wore a big grin, but now that smile had turned to a scowl.

'Really?' Marlene said icily. 'I've come across some fairly preposterous explanations myself.'

Wanda folded her arms. 'Such as?'

'Edgar de Souza's book, *The Winds of Death*,' Marlene said. 'The killer committed the murder by leaping between two trains moving at the same speed. Then he jumped back to the first train again, thereby establishing himself with an alibi.'

'But that's theoretically possible. In this instance, Janice Stella abseiled around the side of the castle before shooting the professor in his study adn then returning to her room to continue playing her violin solo. And all this in under sixty seconds!'

'It's possible.'

'Really? Have you done it lately?'

Uh oh, I thought.

Things were about to get *really* ugly. Once, Marlene may have done many physical things—including abseiling—but those days were over. Marlene owned the local sweet shop, and too much sampling of her wares had put an end to her abseiling days. Just as I was about to intervene, Edward Blayney, the owner of Ed's Pastries, hesitantly raised a hand.

'Perhaps we could ask our resident athlete,' he said. 'Kim?'

I was sitting next to my best friend, Kim Chen. At six feet one, I was a full foot taller than her, but she seemed to shrink even further under Wanda's gaze.

Kim had worked in the library for several years before taking over as Head Librarian after Wanda's retirement. I knew that, even now, Kim sometimes struggled to stand up to her former boss.

'Well,' she said. 'My violin playing is not what it used to be. I did take a few lessons as a kid, but it wasn't for me. I was more of a Nirvana or REM kind of girl. If I could have played their music on violin—' She stopped, realising that she was prattling. 'I think it could be done, but you'd have to be quick. *Really* quick.'

Silence filled the room again. The only sound was that of some children in the central part of the library. A new gaming room had been recently installed and had brought local kids in by the truckload.

'I agree.' This time, the speaker was Doris Glow, one of the club's other members, and the receptionist from the Cape Carson Gazette, where I was a journalist. 'I *have* abseiled, and it's possible. Difficult, but possible.' Considering Doris's age—she was seventy—I could not imagine her abseiling, although, to be fair, she was still in fantastic shape. 'Mind you, that wouldn't be the most difficult part.'

'Really?' Wanda said, surprised.

'Gupman's Violin concerto in D Minor is a hard piece. One of his most difficult.' Her eyes focused on a plate at the side. 'My goodness. Are those homemade lamingtons?'

All eyes swivelled to the table.

'They certainly are,' Nola Evans said.

'Who made those?' Monica Evans asked.

'We did!' Nola said.

'I thought we brought strawberry macarons.'

'That was last week!'

Despite being ninety-six, and living twenty kilometres away

in Port Logan, the sisters never failed to miss a meeting. They owned an old 1955 Dodge La Femme and still drove to Cape Carson at least twice a week.

'Now could be a good time for a tea break,' Kim suggested tactfully.

The group concurred. With World War Three momentarily averted, everyone grabbed a cup of tea or coffee and a lamington.

'You're full of surprises,' I said softly to Doris. 'Abseiling. Violin.'

Doris shrugged. 'I rather liked abseiling,' she said and lowered her voice. 'Mind you, Wanda was right. I've read several of Joel Whitcut's books. They're all the same. Always relying on some ridiculous bit of acrobatics to commit the crime. Even at my best, it would have taken me twice as long.'

'I know what you mean,' I replied. 'It would take me at least an hour. Maybe two. And that's just getting out the window.'

Kim drifted over. 'I never guess the killer,' she grumbled. 'I thought it was the husband.'

I sighed. 'You *always* think it's the husband.'

'Only because it usually is!'

Before I could respond to this, another figure drifted into view. Very few men came to the Cape Carson Mystery Book Club, a shame because it would have been a great place for them to meet women.

Tonight, however, a tall, wiry blonde man with green eyes had attended the meeting. He had a basketballer's physique and moved with an underlying confidence that I found quite attractive.

'Hello ladies,' he said. 'I think it's a shame I didn't read the book. It sounded interesting.'

Kim straightened her dress as I pushed back my hair. Even Doris stood a little straighter.

'It's Keith,' she said. 'Isn't it?'

'Keith Yaeger,' he said. 'I'm in town for a few weeks on business.'

'Rosie Ryan,' I introduced myself.

'Have you read any other Joel Whitcut books?'

'Most of them. I've been busy, though, so I hadn't gotten to this one.'

Keith glanced about. 'Seems a nice group.'

'Oh yes,' I said. My body was having a strange reaction in Keith's presence. Sort of simultaneously hot and cold, and I was feeling all heady. It could have been the first signs of a flu, but I doubted it. 'We're really nice. I mean...very friendly. Not overly friendly,' I hastened to add. 'Not in a weird way. Just...friendly.'

Somehow, Kim and Doris managed not to roll their eyes.

'And a lovely town,' Keith continued, seemingly oblivious to my drooling. He glanced at his watch. 'I'd better get moving.

Great meeting you all.'

Wishing us a goodnight, he left, leaving me to deal with Doris and Kim.

Kim turned to me. 'Very friendly?'

'Not in a weird way?' Doris added.

I shook my head. 'I hate you both.'

They burst out laughing. It was getting late now, so I decided to leave. I reached my jeep, half-hoping that Keith might have been hanging around, but the street was deserted. A few minutes later, I was pulling into the driveway of the house that I shared with my grandmother.

I staggered through the front door, unsuccessfully stifling a yawn as my beagle, Trixie, came bounding up. Giving her a pat, I continued on to the living room.

'You're sounding tired,' Nan commented.

She and her grey-bearded boyfriend Dave were curled up on the lounge watching television.

'It's been a long day.' My gaze crossed to a young boy on the screen. 'That's not what I think it is, is it?'

'If you guessed Home Alone,' Dave said. 'You'd be wrong.'

'It's The Shining,' Nan added.

I groaned. 'You're kidding,' I said. 'Kim's been trying to get me to watch that for years.'

'It's really thrilling, although I think my hair is greyer now as a result.'

'Horror is *not* my thing.'

'By the way,' Nan said, fixing me with her steely eyes. 'What are you doing about the boatshed?'

'The one down at the bay?'

Recently, there'd been an uproar when the publicly owned building was purchased by local businessman Giuseppe Costa. He'd submitted a council application to have it bulldozed and a whole new building constructed. Most of the town wanted it to remain as is. The boatshed was over a century old and was almost as much a part of Cape Carson's history as the lighthouse.

'What other boatshed is there?' Nan asked, momentarily ignoring the thousands of other boatsheds around Australia. 'You're not going to let Giuseppe get away with it, are you?'

'Nan. I'm a journalist. Not the Prime Minister.'

'Thank goodness for that because he couldn't find his own—'

'And my job is to report the news—'

'—and not be it. You've told me that a hundred times. Now you listen to me, Rosie Ryan. Giuseppe Costa already owns half the properties up and down the coast. He's been fined by the council at least twice for violating building codes. We can't let him get away with this. The people of this town need to stand up and be counted.'

'Maybe, but I'm ready to lie down, and the only thing I'm

ready to count is sheep,' I said. 'See you in the morning.'

I headed off to bed and closed my door to shut out the ominous sounds from the television. Trixie took up her spot on the floor beside my bed.

'Goodnight, Trixie,' I said.

I was asleep within seconds. The dreams that came consisted of me being locked in the tower of a castle. Unable to escape, I peered out the window in dismay until I spotted a shadowy figure scaling the rocky wall towards me. When he reached the open window, I was surprised to see he had blonde hair and green eyes.

'Keith?' I said in amazement.

'You were expecting someone else?'

Drrriiiinnnggg!

I opened my eyes.

Morning already? I snapped off my alarm. I hardly felt like I'd been to bed.

I got ready, ate some breakfast, and was sitting at my desk an hour later.

The story I was working on was about Unicorn Books, a Cape Carson second-hand bookshop that was celebrating its fiftieth anniversary. I let out a yawn.

'Not enough sleep?' Jay enquired.

He shared the small office at the back of the building with me.

'It's that obvious?' I asked.

'I think you forgot to brush your hair.'

'Huh?'

I pulled out a mirror from my handbag, muttered something under my breath, and brushed my hair into shape. Doris appeared in the doorway with an envelope.

'Rosie,' she said. 'You've got mail.'

'Really?' I said. 'The old-fashioned kind? Does that still happen?'

'It's a rarity.'

Doris handed me the envelope.

I glanced at the front and frowned. My name was typed using an old-fashioned typewriter. I turned it over. There was no return address. I tore it open and extracted a single piece of paper folded once in half. The page was light blue with a double-orange line running across the top.

On it was typed:

So strange, all these deaths in Port Logan. And now, Stewart Bard.

2

I leaned into Harry Blackshore's office. 'Got a minute?' I asked.

'What is it?' Harry was working on the business accounts for the paper. He hated doing it, but it was one of his roles as the owner and Editor-In-Chief. 'You look serious, and I don't like your serious face.'

I handed the note to him.

'No return address?' he asked after reading it.

'None.'

'And it arrived today?'

I nodded. 'Doris gave it to me.' I showed Harry the envelope. 'It could be a hoax. You know, nothing, but maybe...'

'It might be something.'

What that something could be was still a mystery. Harry sat back from his computer. 'Refresh my memory, Rosie,' he said. 'Stewart Bard. Wasn't that the guy who got crushed in a rockfall?'

'At Port Logan,' I confirmed.

I'd written the story myself. There hadn't been a whole lot to it. That whole section of coast was notoriously unstable. Sometimes days of torrential rain resulted in landslides. A man had been on his early morning walk when a rock dislodged, and he was crushed beneath it.

Harry reread the note. '*All these deaths in Port Logan,*' he said. 'Does that sound right?'

'I don't know,' I said, thinking hard. 'There have been a few. I don't recall the details.'

'And you know who most people would blame?'

I groaned. 'Good grief. Not the Port Logan monster?'

'People have been talking about a Port Logan monster for years,' he said. 'It's the stuff of local legend.'

More like complete rubbish than local legend. I'd first heard of the monster when I visited Cape Carson as a kid.

'There's no sea monster,' I said. 'It's a complete fantasy.'

'Sometimes legends contain a grain of truth. Maybe something is going on at Port Logan.' He paused. 'This could be worth following up, and things are quiet here at the moment. Jay can help cover some of your other stories.'

'Sure.' Although zooming off to Port Logan wasn't something I relished, there might be something in this. Or not. The whole thing could be a hoax cooked up by someone's overactive imagination. 'It might take a few days.'

'Or you might have it sewn up in an afternoon.'

Port Logan wasn't my favourite place. I don't think anyone liked it much. Maybe not even the people who lived there. It was only in recent years that the council had allowed some of the old places to be demolished and new homes built. Even then, the cost of building around Port Logan bay was hellishly expensive because of the deep foundations that had to be sunk to stabilise the buildings. After telling Harry I'd keep him in the loop, I returned to my desk and finished the story about the bookshop. Then I turned to Jay and told him that I was heading down to Port Logan for a few days.

'Really?' he said. 'You're looking into the monster?'

I did an eye roll. 'Not the monster.'

'Not a believer?'

'Definitely not. I don't believe in sea monsters.'

I continued working on a story I'd been writing about the local boatshed. Nan had been right about something. People were up in arms about it. I filled in some of the remaining details before sending the story to Jay. 'Most of this is background stuff,' I said. 'Can you give this a quick edit before sending it to Harry?'

Jay glanced at the article. 'Do you think council will approve Giuseppe's redevelopment?'

'I hope not. There's already too much bulldozing going on around here.'

I turned my attention to Steward Bard. The story I'd written for the Gazette wouldn't win me any Wakely awards.

Everything I'd had to say amounted to half a column on page three, and that was because the information had come straight from the Cape Carson police.

Stewart Bard's death had happened shortly before the new sergeant—Todd Parker—had started. Although he might have given it more attention than his infamously neglectful predecessor, I doubted anyone would have looked twice at it.

Even I hadn't thought it suspicious. Rockfalls happened. Not all the time. Maybe twice a year. It was unusual, though, that someone was killed by one.

My article hadn't even included a photo of the accident site. Just a generic picture that we'd pulled from our photo archive. Printing a copy of the article, I said a quick goodbye to everyone and headed out the door with Trixie by my side. We made our way to my old jeep and climbed in.

I gave Kim a ring to see if she wanted to tag along. The library was being renovated, which meant her hours were more flexible than usual.

'A trip to Port Logan?' her voice came back dubiously on the phone. 'Can't we do Paris or London? Even Sydney would do.'

'I'm afraid not.' I quickly told her about the letter. 'There's a chance Stewart Bard was murdered.'

'Ah-ha. The monster strikes again.'

'Not the monster!'

'Yes! The monster! Just because you don't believe doesn't mean it's not real.' She paused. 'Anyway, you know I love a good murder. Pick me up from the library in ten.'

Fortunately, Kim enjoyed investigating murders and not committing them. Our friendship never would have worked if it had been the other way around. I did as she requested, and we were soon cruising back down to Percy street.

The day was bright and clear, and the bay bordering our little seaside town was flat. Boats moored at the wharf sat silent and still. I glanced up and down the street. There weren't many people about. Cape Carson needed tourists—I knew that—but I couldn't help but feel a sense of satisfaction when I recognised only familiar faces on the street.

'Coffee?' Kim suggested.

'Is the Pope a Catholic?' I answered.

I pulled over at Sandy's Diner. A group of surfers sat around the front tables, their boards leaning against the walls.

'Wait here,' I said.

I hurried inside to grab our usual coffees: Kim drank a skim cappuccino while I ordered my usual jumbo double-shot caramel latte. A few people worked at the rock and roll themed diner, but no one made a better coffee than the owner herself. Sandy was a buxom woman with short blonde hair and more than a few tattoos. As she frothed the milk for our coffees, I told her where we were heading.

'Port Logan?' she said. 'Isn't everyone there feral?'

I laughed. 'At least you're not warning me about the sea monster.'

'I'm not worried about the monster. I don't want you getting bitten by any of the locals.'

Port Logan was often the butt of jokes. 'Not everyone in Port Logan is feral,' I said, and told her about Monica and Nola. 'They're lovely old ladies.'

'And still chipper at ninety-six?' Sandy said, handing me the coffees. 'You obviously don't know a vampire when you see one.'

Laughing, I paid and returned to the jeep. From there, we drove out of town, past the lighthouse, and on to Millicent Drive. The road bordering West Beach was long and flat, with gaps between the sand dunes affording me glimpses of the ocean. The water had started to turn choppy.

Looks like the weather's changing, I thought.

It didn't take long to reach Port Logan.

Turning off Millicent drive, I followed a dirt road up and over a sharp rise. I stopped next to a road sign reading *Oxley Street* and peered down into the small bay beyond.

The whole area was a tiny, hilly inlet with fewer than a dozen houses adjoining the coastal path and road. The buildings were an eclectic mix, mostly rundown beach shacks nestled beside soaring mansions made of glass and steel. These must have been the places that had cost so much to build.

It's amazing what people will do for a water view, I thought.

An odd mix of vessels were moored at Port Logan's tiny jetty. A luxurious sports cruiser sat among the few old timber boats, one of which was sunk and another desperately overdue for a coat of paint.

The bay's ground was rocky and dry, although some ragged-looking trees had survived against the relentless on-shore breeze. A few of the beach shacks had veggie gardens. In the main street sat a general store, although it was hard to tell if it was open or not.

'Still as cheery as always,' Kim said. 'If you ever have feelings of dire hopelessness, this is the place to come and confirm them.'

'It's not that bad.'

'It's worse. No wonder the monster took up residence here.' Trixie whined.

'Not the monster, Kim,' I groaned. 'And what's this thing supposed to look like? Is it like the Loch Ness monster? Or bigfoot? Or—'

'I've got a picture.' She started searching her phone. 'I took it years ago when I came over here on a picnic.'

Kim finally found the image and showed it to me. The photo

was of her and her ex-husband at the beach. A dark shape lay in the water behind.

'That could be anything,' I said. 'Anyway, let's get moving. We won't learn anything sitting up here.'

We drove down the hill and pulled up in front of the general store. Close up, the old beach shacks looked slightly better, but not much. They were all timber places that needed either a paint job or a wrecking ball. The few new constructions that had gone up made them look even worse.

I wonder where Nola and Monica live.

Kim must have been reading my mind as she gripped my arm.

'Look,' she murmured. 'That's Monica and Nola's car.'

It was indeed. The rear end of the old 1955 Dodge La Femme was sticking out of a garage of one of the less ramshackle timber homes. Other than the washed-out pink and milk-white paint job, the car was in good shape. I shook my head in admiration. Some of those old cars were notoriously difficult to drive. At least the road from here to Cape Carson was good and as straight as a die. Plus, they'd probably done the trip so many thousands of times over the years that they could have driven it blindfolded.

The sign over the front of the general store read *Kelly's General Store*. I'd visited it once years before when I'd taken a wrong turn and stopped off for a chocolate bar.

It'd been a memorable experience for all the wrong reasons. The chocolate had been old, dry, and a year out of date.

Despite these minor details, I'd still eaten it. After all, bad chocolate's still chocolate.

Right?

'We could drop in on the twins,' Kim suggested.

'I don't want to do that unannounced. They might be...' Actually, I wasn't sure what Nola and Monica did in their spare time. I remembered Sandy's comments about vampires. Saying they might be sleeping in the middle of the day sounded a little too undead for my liking. 'They might be taking a walk. Or something. Let's try the general store.'

'Is it open?'

'Sure,' I said, glancing at the grubby building. 'I think.'

Opening the screen door of the general store revealed a tired-looking interior. Fluorescent lights ran down the centre. Refrigerators emblazoned with Coke advertising were at one end with a counter at the other.

The sparsely packed shelves were dusty and disordered. I spotted a cereal packet with advertising for a movie that had come out last year.

The woman behind the counter looked as tired as her shop. She was undoubtedly the same person who had served me years ago. She was fifty, pasty-faced, with dyed black hair and a troll-like body. She didn't so much sit at the counter as slump over it, a women's magazine in hand, and a half-ravaged packet of Tim Tams at her elbow.

I introduced myself, told her Kim was my photographer and said I was interested in doing a story about the town.

'What about it?' she asked.

Well, that was the sixty-four dollar question, really. What was there to tell about this horrible little town with its single claim to fame being a monster that wanted to eat you?

'A story about the town's history,' I clarified. 'Port Logan's been here a long time.' When the woman looked at me without speaking, I continued. 'An article would bring more people to the town and your business.'

'Really?'

Although, they won't stay long once they see your shop. Most people will probably run a mile.

'Absolutely,' I said, smiling. 'You're Mrs Kelly?'

'Iris Kelly.'

Great. At least now we were on a first-name basis. I asked if she knew how many people lived in Port Logan.

'Not many,' she said. 'Less than a dozen. Even fewer now.'

'Even fewer?' I asked

'We had a death here recently: Stewart Bard.'

I nodded. 'He was killed in a rockfall?'

'Yep.'

This was like getting blood from a stone. Kim, in the meantime, had zoomed around the shelves and picked up some provisions. At the sight of actually making a purchase, Iris seemed to perk up a little. Maybe this was the biggest sale she'd make all day. Maybe all week.

'How did that come about?' I asked. 'The rockfall, I mean.'

'There was rain,' Iris said as she tallied the items. 'Days of it. The ground around the cliffs gets soggy. It's dangerous walking around them. Doesn't stop stupid people, though. They get told, but they still do it.'

'Where did the accident happen?' I asked. 'Exactly.'

The headlands at the entrance to the bay were called East and West Head. She described a section of coast two hundred metres past East Head. The woman then continued to say that there'd been rockfalls along this section of the coast for years.

'I don't recall anyone getting killed before,' I said.

'No,' Iris agreed thoughtfully as Kim paid for her groceries. 'Stewart was the first.'

After telling her I'd drop back in later to ask a few more questions, Kim and I headed out to the car. Trixie gave an anxious yowl.

'We're okay, girl,' I said, ruffling her neck. 'We survived the witch's lair.' I turned to Kim. 'What'd you buy?'

'Just the essentials: chocolates, biscuits, bags of lollies.'

'How do you stay skinny?'

'Pact with the devil. I'm spending eternity as a toasted

marshmallow.'

'Bummer.'

Kim threw the essentials into the back of the jeep. I was about to suggest that we go for a walk around the headland when the front door of Nola and Monica's house was flung open.

'Hello!' Nola called. 'Monica! Guess who's come to town!'

Monica's voice came from inside. 'Is it our nephew John?'

'No! He died in 1984! It's Kim and Rosie!'

'Who?'

'From the book club.'

Monica appeared, and we gave the pair a wave and wandered over. At first glance, I'd thought their garden looked somewhat disorganised. However, on closer inspection, I realised there was a kind of rough beauty to their yard. It was full of coastal succulents that grew wild in the area. Their house was bigger than I'd first thought too. It was a one storey home jutting out from the hill with what appeared to be a vast basement below.

'What brings you here?' Monica asked. 'Are you lost? That road can be quite tricky.'

Considering the road was dead straight, the last thing I would have described it as was tricky.

'We've over here doing a story,' Kim said.

'Not about all the deaths?' Nola asked.

Ah-ha, I thought.

I'd made the same mistake as a lot of people. It was easy to think of Nola and Monica Evans as two senile old ladies. Easy, until I remembered that they successfully picked the killer in around half the books we studied at book club. That was a good batting average. Better than mine.

'Deaths?' I said, deciding to play dumb. 'How do you mean?'

Nola tapped the side of her nose. 'We've been watching,' she said in a low voice. 'Haven't we, Monica?'

'We have. A lot of people have died of late.'

'But we've kept it to ourselves.'

'Otherwise, they might think we're crazy,' Monica said.

'Crazy!' Nola added, with a cackling laugh that did nothing to dispel that notion.

I wasn't sure how all this huddling together on the street would look to the neighbours. Everyone could more or less see each other in this tiny inlet. For all I knew, half the town was peering out from behind their curtains, wondering why we were being so conspiratorial.

'All right,' I said carefully. 'Kim and I are making a few inquiries, but it must be all kept hush-hush. We'll talk more later.'

'We understand,' Monica said. 'Hush-hush.'

'Hush-hush,' Nola agreed.

I told her we were taking a walk around East Head to see

where Stewart Bard had died. The ladies nodded knowingly and said they were available to chat anytime. They headed inside.

'They're not as dizzy as they seem,' Kim said, thoughtfully.

'Not at all.'

'Could they have sent you the letter?'

'I don't see why they would. They know I never reveal my sources.'

The path led in both directions around the tiny cove. We turned left, following as it trailed along the front of the houses.

I was more aware than ever of the windows surrounding us. It was hard to believe that anyone could get murdered here without the entire town noticing.

Coming around East Head, an onshore breeze washed over us, and I felt an odd sense of relief.

'You feel that too?' Kim said.

'You bet. That's one weird town.'

From here, we could see the coast receding away in both directions. Beyond West Head lay Cullen beach, and past that, a series of headlands that disappeared into a fine blue-grey line. In the other direction was Piper beach, and a jutting out spot I recognised as Point Gower. It obscured our view of West Beach and Cape Carson beyond.

We continued along the path, the ocean below us, vast and deep. The wind had picked up, and the waves were capped with white. At times like this, I tried to imagine what was going on beneath the water's surface. That great, heaving, breathing mass, filled with billions of tiny creatures, as oblivious to me as I was to them.

If I'd felt any concern about finding the spot where Stewart Bard died, my fears would have been unfounded. The boulder had struck the path, collapsing a section before slamming into the rocky platform below. It had come from the very top of the high cliff above. Safely wedged in that position for hundreds of years, it had dislodged just at the moment when Stewart Bard was passing below. The section of path it had struck was a sharp hairpin turn, making it impossible to avoid the boulder.

The council had since put barricade tape across the path, but it was unnecessary. The trail was still navigable, and the ground seemed to have settled completely.

'Let's take a look around the top,' I suggested.

'It's too steep to climb here,' Kim said. 'The track might angle up around the other side.'

She was correct. Scrambling over the tape and continuing around the next cliff, we found the track divided in two. One trailed ahead in the direction of the rock platform bordering the water. The other took us up the hill along a sandy path surrounded by low-lying saltbush and spinifex.

The rear fences of houses backed onto the top of the hill. Most of the fences were in a terrible state. Port Logan was so quiet that owners probably didn't worry too much about security.

Kim pointed to a gap in the rock where the boulder had dislodged. I peered into the void. It was warm in the sun, and yet I felt cold.

How long had that boulder sat there? Hundreds of years? And how many people traipsed along that lonely coastal path? Although it was probably busier during midsummer, maybe only a handful of people used it at this time of year. What were the chances of the boulder dislodging just as someone passed below?

'What do you think?' I asked Kim.

She knelt beside the hole. 'Look at this,' she said, pointing to the spot where the rock had broken away. 'That *could* be the mark of a crowbar.'

It was a tiny, sharp cleft. 'Or it could be just a mark.'

'Maybe.'

We returned to the path, this time taking it across the grassy hill to where it met Oxley Street. Soon, we were ensconced back in my jeep, where we cracked open one of the packets of chocolate biscuits. True to form, they were stale, but I didn't care.

'I need to interview some people,' I said. 'One of them is Stewart Bard's wife, Sybil.'

I remembered her name from the original police report.

'And who else?'

'Todd.' I took a long breath. 'I want to know what the police made of this accident.'

3

'Rosie,' Jay said. 'I need to list some things after a sentence. Is that a colon or semicolon?'

'It's the one indicated by the grammar book I got you for your birthday,' I said, without glancing up from my laptop. 'But if you left that at home, you should use a colon.'

'Thanks, Rosie.'

'That's fine. Bring the grammar book to work.'

'Okay.'

I put the finishing touches on my notes and glanced at my watch. Almost four o'clock. That was too late for coffee. Or was it? Surely there was no arbiter who determined how much coffee a person should drink. I was a grown woman! I could drink as much coffee as I wanted!

Grabbing my bag, I headed out past Doris's desk with Trixie at my side.

Harry yelled from his office. 'Rosie? Are you getting coffee?'

'No,' I called back. 'It's straight gin all the way.'

'Good. Too much coffee's bad for you.'

Grumbling, I headed out the door and onto the footpath. 'What does he know?' I asked Trixie, who replied with a small bark. 'Exactly. Harry should be smart enough to never get between a woman and her caffeine.'

Heading down Percy Street, I was almost at Sandy's when I spotted a familiar person exiting a shop. My ex-husband, George, had moved back to Cape Carson after our breakup. A few years before, seeing him would have brought on an argument, but our marriage had been over long enough for us to reach a kind of détente. Although we weren't friends, we weren't enemies either, and that was bearable.

George's face flushed. 'Hey Rosie,' he said. 'Big surprise.'

'Yeah. Sure.' I stared at him. When you've been married to someone for a long time, you can tell when something's wrong. George looked downright uncomfortable. As if I'd found him doing something naughty. 'How're you doing?'

'Great.' He glanced into the shop. 'Going somewhere?'

That question was both odd and stupid. Surely everyone was going somewhere in some form. 'Just out for coffee.'

A woman left the shop. 'I ended up getting the—' she stopped. 'Oh—hi.'

'Hello,' I said.

She was shorter than me, maybe around forty, with a big head of brown hair and wearing a formfitting dress.

'This is Sadie,' George said.

He didn't follow it up with any more information, so the first thing that went through my mind was the line from an old song, *Sadie, the Cleaning Lady*. This lady may have been named Sadie, but she was no cleaning lady.

I introduced myself and mustered up a smile. 'Don't tell me you're hanging out with this layabout,' I said.

Sadie countered. 'I am,' she said. 'Good men are hard to come by.'

Oh well, I thought. *At least she's got a sense of humour.*

'You live in Cape Carson?' I asked.

'With George.'

Goodness. That was quick.

The fact that she said George and not *George and Nico* meant they were in a relationship. Nico was George's brother, and George and his previous girlfriend, Blossom, had been staying with Nico for some time. It looked like Blossom had been replaced by Sadie.

It wasn't altogether surprising. George and Blossom had been on the outer the last time I heard. It sounded like *outer* had become *over*, although it appeared George had been quick to survive his broken heart.

'You should come over for dinner,' Sadie said.

I nodded, thinking I could imagine nothing worse.

'Bring your boyfriend,' George suggested.

Boyfriend?

This left me genuinely mystified until I realised he was talking about Todd, who definitely wasn't my boyfriend. We'd been out on a few dates and enjoyed a nice walk on a moonlit beach. Other than that, our relationship had gone nowhere. With him being a cop, and me a journalist, our careers placed us on the opposite side of the same fence.

Still, I didn't want to look like the ditched wife who couldn't get on with her life.

'Sure,' I said. 'I'll ask him.'

We set up a time and date.

Wishing them a good day, I headed down the street, my stomach a cauldron of mixed emotions. Instead of heading to Sandy's Diner for coffee, I made my way to the police station on First Avenue. Although the Cape Carson Police Station wasn't one of the most outstanding places in town, it was one of the most historic. Over a hundred years old, the tin roof had been recently replaced, although the red bricks on the side were original. I'd been here a lot over the years. Back in the old days, it was Todd's predecessor, Sergeant Wilson, that I'd be interviewing. He was never helpful. At least Todd was an improvement.

Constable Jim Turner, tall and gangly with brown hair, was staffing the counter. He stowed away a gaming magazine as I entered.

'I saw that,' I informed him. 'Are you still playing that game?'

'What game?'

'What's it called? Flying Steamships in Cucumber Land?'

He grimaced. '*A Steamcar in Dinosaur Town*,' he said. 'It's a cooperative board game that allows you to take control of the world after civilisation has fallen and dinosaurs rule the earth once more.'

'What a relief. I thought it was something nerdy.'

'Well, you were wrong.'

He'd obviously not picked up on my sarcasm. 'Can I see Todd Parker?' I asked.

'Only if you promise never to mock my board game again.'

'I promise on the skull of Lord Tyrannosaurus Steamhead that I will never mock your game again.'

Despite this last comment, Jim let me through to see Todd. The well-built sergeant was focused on his computer screen, his brow furrowed as he typed two-fingered. He grunted a greeting as I sat.

'Having a good time?' I asked.

'Wonderful. A kid steals another kid's skateboard, and I have to file a five thousand page report. What can I do for you?'

I asked what he knew about Stewart Bard's death.

He looked up from the computer. 'Hmm. Not a lot. It was a little before my time,' he said. 'Peter Wilson handled it.'

'There wasn't any follow-up?'

'There was no need for it.' He obligingly, but very slowly because of his typing speed, brought up a file on his computer. 'There were three other rockfalls up and down the coast that week. Someone else broke a leg when a path collapsed. The death at Port Logan was ruled an accident.'

'Bit of bad luck that Stewart Bard just happened to be on the path.'

'Bad luck happens.' He studied my face. 'Why do you ask? It's not because of the sea monster?'

'You've heard about that?'

'Everyone seems to have a story about it.'

'Everyone other than me.' I wasn't about to tell him that I was investigating this because of an anonymous tip. The media and police received those all the time, and they often led to nothing. 'I'm doing a history piece on the town.' *Well, that's partially true.* 'By the way, how are your evenings looking?'

'Only eating and sleeping.' He raised an eyebrow. 'Did you have something else in mind?'

A rather pleasant spark of electricity ran down my body as a myriad of possibilities crossed my mind. I brought my hormones under control. 'Down boy,' I said. 'My ex-husband and his new hussy have invited me for dinner. I thought you might like to come.'

'That's quite an invitation.' He leaned back in his seat. 'Am

I the first person you asked?'

'As a matter of fact, you are.'

'In that case, the answer is yes. Should I bring anything?'

'Patience.' I gave him the details. 'I'm not sure how much fun it'll be.'

'That's the most gracious invitation I've received in ages, which says a lot about my social life.' He paused. 'I have a favour to ask.'

'Yes?'

He leaned closer and lowered his voice. 'I'd prefer you don't mention the Rusty Jones Mysteries.'

'What?' Todd had been the star of the kid's TV show when he was young. 'But that's your claim to fame.'

'And that's why I don't want it mentioned. That was all a long time ago, and I don't want to be reminded of that life.'

I gave a slow nod, understanding Todd's reticence. From the few conversations we'd had, I knew he had mixed feelings about his acting career. His father had been the driving force behind everything he did, and Todd hadn't spoken to him for some time.

Thanking him, I headed out of the office with Trixie and back down to Percy Street. The day was cooling. Despite there being no sign of rain on the horizon, I still felt like there was a change in the air.

My phone rang: Harry.

'Rosie?' he said. 'I've got a contact you might be interested in.'

'Is it a number for the Chippendales? I've always wanted to interview those guys.'

'It's better: Sybil Bard.'

'Stewart's wife?'

'Turns out that Ellie here at the office slightly knows her. Sybil owns the garden centre in Crawley Street.'

Ellie was the dreadlocked and nose-pierced IT guru in our office. She and a group of people lived in a commune a few kilometres inland. Maybe she'd bought plants from Sybil.

'Fantastic,' I said. 'I'll head over there now.'

It was late, but hopefully the centre would still be open. A few minutes later, Trixie and I were pulling up outside. There were two nurserys in town and—I'm sorry to say—this was the one less frequented. The Crawley Street Garden Centre was a few blocks from the main road. The other one was more centrally located and a local institution.

Sybil was alone in her shop as if desperate for a customer. I quickly noticed a maidenhair fern near the entrance. I'd always loved those plants but never owned one before. Picking it up, I strode over and plonked it on the counter. The woman's face perceptibly brightened. After paying, I told her the other reason for my visit.

'You're interested in Stewart's death?' she said. 'Why?'

I didn't want to mention the anonymous letter.

'I'm doing a story about Port Logan,' I said. 'It's often seen as the neglected cousin of Cape Carson. I thought I could bring some much-needed attention to the town.'

'I wouldn't want Stewart's death sensationalised.'

'And that's not my intention. The human story behind his passing might give the town a better image.'

'I see.'

For a long time, I thought she was going to ask me to leave, but then she motioned to a nearby garden setting, and we sat.

'Stewart and I moved to Port Logan about eight years ago,' Sybil said. 'We both trained as chemists but wanted to try something different. We sold our business in Melbourne and moved here. While we'd intended to live in Cape Carson, we moved to Port Logan because it was quieter.'

'It is a tiny town,' I agreed. 'I suppose everyone knows everyone else.'

'More's the pity,' Sybil said.

I asked her what she meant.

'Do you know Ray Pennington?' she asked.

'I'm afraid not.'

Sybil groaned. 'If you talk to him, he'll bore you to death about his family coming over with the First Fleet. Unfortunately, he owns half the town.'

'Really?'

'Most of the abandoned beach shacks are owned by him. He's got no money to fix them up.'

Asset rich and dollar poor, I thought. *And it's notoriously difficult to get new developments passed by the council because of the unstable ground.*

'Can you tell me how Stewart's accident came about?' I asked.

Sybil sighed. 'It happened just after those storms that came through a few months back. They went on for days, and you know what the coast is like. There's always rock falls and areas that are considered unsafe.

'That made no difference to Stewart. He never missed his morning walk. We've been struggling with this business for a long time. The walk helped him to clear his mind. One morning he headed out...' She swallowed. 'He was gone about twenty minutes when I heard a distant crash. I thought it was thunder at first. Then Grace Vickery came racing up to the house.'

'She's a local?'

'Yes. Lives across the bay. Even before she spoke, I knew there was something horribly wrong.' Sybil looked down at her hands. 'She'd been on a walk when she heard the boulder come down. Grace went to take a look and saw where it had hit the path. Then she saw blood...'

Sybil's voice trailed away to nothing.

'Have there been any other accidents on that section of coast?' I asked gently.

'A few. No one's been killed, though.'

'I suppose people pass away rarely in a place like Port Logan.'

Sybil looked at me suddenly. 'Well,' she said. 'It's strange you say that. There have been a few deaths over the last year or so.'

'Really?'

'Yes. Someone was talking about it the other day. There was Stewart, of course, but before him, there was Cynthia.'

'Cynthia?'

'Cynthia Shepherd. She fell over on her boat and died.'

'Fell over? Did she hit her head?'

'No. Cynthia fell on her knife.'

'Goodness.'

'It was a freak accident. Cynthia wasn't young, though. Maybe seventy. Maybe she was getting a bit too old to be scrambling about on boats. She was a tough old thing, though. She used to take her little boat out off the coast and do some fishing. One morning, someone noticed her boat wasn't tied up properly. They went on board to check and found her dead.'

'When did that happen?'

'About six months back.'

'And before that?'

Sybil thought. 'There's one...no, two that come to mind.

That horrible Jamie Farrell. I know it's wrong to speak ill of the dead, but it's amazing he lived as long as he did. He was a delinquent. If it wasn't graffiti, it was vandalism or just plain old being an obnoxious pest. It was tragic for his parents but a blessing for everyone else.'

'So everyone was kind of glad—'

Sybil laughed for the first time. 'Hey,' she said. 'Don't put words into my mouth. The kid was seventeen. It was a terrible thing. And there may have been something wrong with his brain. If there were, his parents have never said anything about it. He was an odd little loner. Getting drunk all the time. He broke into Philip Taylor's home and stole some alcohol. He'd also gotten some illegal drugs from somewhere. Jamie went up into the dunes, knocked back a cocktail mix of both, and died.'

'My goodness,' I said, counting. 'That's three deaths.'

Trixie whined in agreement.

'It's a lot,' Sybil agreed. 'I suppose that can happen, though. Of course, some people have even mentioned the monster. You've probably heard that story?'

I nodded.

'It's rubbish, of course,' she continued. 'I've never seen any-thing. People just don't live a long time in Port Logan.'

'There are the Evans twins,' I pointed out.

Sybil laughed again. 'You know them?' she said. 'Yes, they're the exception to the rule. Stewart always used to call them vampires. Not to their faces, of course.' She shook her head. 'Sorry, I sound awful. They're lovely ladies but hard to take in big doses. We had them for dinner one night, and they spent the whole evening talking about their favourite mystery writers. It was almost Christmas by the time we shuffled them out the door.'

'You mentioned two other deaths. One was Jamie Farrell. Who was the other?'

'It was an old friend of Grace Vickery's,' Sybil said, thoughtfully. 'It must be almost two years ago now. The woman had just arrived from insterstate on the bus. She was killed in a hit and run on the crest of the road where you turn off to come down the hill.'

This death didn't sound like the others. Everyone else who died was a local. This other woman had barely even made it to town before dying. Her death could be unrelated—if any of them were related at all. This was four people dead in the space of two years. Statistically, that seemed like a high number for a tiny spot like Port Logan.

Unless something else was at work...

That's ridiculous, I thought. *The Port Logan Monster is not real!*

At least, I didn't think it was.

A car pulled into the garden centre's parking lot.

'Looks like you've got a customer,' I said. 'May I give you a call if I have any other questions?'

'Sure,' Sybil said. 'And thanks for buying the maidenhair. Remember: don't let it dry out. They love lots of moisture.' She walked a few feet with me before stopping. 'I hope you can do Stewart justice. He was a great husband, and I loved him dearly. I miss him every day.'

I promised to treat his memory with respect.

Trixie and I returned to my jeep, where I wondered what the best course of action would be.

'Trixie,' I said. 'I'm going to talk to Nola and Monica Evans. You know them: the ladies from the Mystery Book Club.'

Trixie whined.

'I know they're a handful,' I said. 'Good news is that we won't face them alone.'

4

'You're in luck,' Monica said. 'I've been making cookies.'

'No one cooks like Monica,' Nola said. 'She's a master in the kitchen.'

Kim and I were in their Port Logan living room. It was the most crowded home that I'd ever seen. There were sideboards, cupboards, coffee tables, dressers, and bookshelves, configured to create pathways through all the furniture. The paths were so slim that only one person at a time could navigate down them.

Adding to the clutter were ceramic figurines that took up every free square inch of space. The twins seemed to have spent a lifetime collecting them.

'My goodness,' Kim said, glancing about. 'I'm going to guess that someone likes ornaments.'

'Whatever gives you that idea?' Nola said.

'Yes!' Monica said. 'How do you know?'

'Yes, Kim,' I said, feigning innocence. 'Tell us.'

Kim shot me a look of *I'm going to kill you*. 'Just a feeling,' she said.

'And here's your lovely dog,' Nola said. 'What a beautiful beagle.'

Trixie happily wagged her tail, and I slipped her a homemade doggy snack.

I did a quick count of thirty-three figures crammed onto one side table. There was literally no room for anything else.

Nola went to the kitchen and returned a moment later with one of the biggest plates of cookies I'd ever seen. 'Goodness,' I said. 'How many people are you expecting?'

'Monica's a greedy guts,' Nola said.

'She's the greedy guts,' Monica said. 'I went looking for some walnut cake, and she'd eaten it all.'

'We finished that last month!'

I bit into the cookie. 'This is lovely,' I said, keen to divert the conversation. 'You mentioned some deaths in the area.'

'A lot of people have died,' Nola said. 'Stewart and Cynthia.'

'And Grace's friend. I forget her name. And Jamie Farrell, though he was horrible.'

'Horrible.' Nola shuddered. 'Always spray painting things. I don't know where he got the money.'

'Still,' Monica said, 'he didn't deserve to die.'

'Oh no,' Nola agreed. 'He just needed to be put into the army for a while. A good war would have straightened him out. You remember my cousin Stan? He went into the army and—'

Kim cut in. 'So a lot of people have died.'

'There's usually one every five or ten years,' Nola said. 'A small place like this. Around the turn of the century, there were three in one year, but that was the Miller family. They died in a car crash.'

'And these recent deaths look like accidents?' I confirmed.

'Oh, yes,' Monica said. 'They *look* like accidents. Maybe they even *are* accidents. Statistical anomalies do happen. You can get a spike in numbers.'

'That's what the man said on that show on the ABC,' Nola said. 'That mathematician. He was very clever.'

'And handsome,' Monica added wistfully. 'But so many have died here in Port Logan that it makes you wonder if there really is a monster.'

Trixie took refuge under my seat. 'Don't worry, girl,' I said. 'No monster's getting you.' I turned to the ladies. 'Have you ever seen anything odd?'

Although Monica hadn't, Nola said she'd once seen something in the water. 'It was about five years back. A dark shape came to the surface, looked about, and then disappeared.'

'Could it have been a whale?' I asked. 'Or even a dolphin?'

'Maybe,' Nola said sagely. 'But maybe not.'

'There have been a lot of deaths,' Monica continued. 'Oh—Florence! That was the name of Grace's friend.'

'That was so tragic.'

'Florence Teale?' I'd looked her up in the newspaper records. 'She came here for a holiday, I believe?'

'Only just arrived on the evening bus from Melbourne,' Nola said. 'Came all this way, got off the bus and then—*wham*! Hit by a car! Killed instantly, the police said.'

'So terrible for Grace. Distraught, she was. Had been looking forward to seeing her old friend,' Monica said. 'They never caught the driver, and they found the car burnt out later.'

Grace's friend seems to have been the first person to die.

'There's been such tragedy in poor Grace's life,' Monica said. 'She lost her sister a few years back. Very sad.'

'Are you investigating the monster?' Nola asked, sitting her tea down.

'I'm doing some research on Port Logan,' I said carefully. 'Since I started, I heard about the deaths, and I'm curious to know more. What can you tell me about the locals? You mentioned this woman, Grace?'

'Grace Vickery. She moved to Port Logan about ten years ago. A nice woman. Lives next to Ray Pennington.'

'Then there's Philip Taylor,' Monica said. 'He lives a few houses up. Used to work as a gynaecologist.'

'Not a gynaecologist,' Nola said. 'An archaeologist.'

'That's right. Different kind of mummies!' The old ladies burst out laughing. 'Anyway, he's lived here about five years. Retired young because he had some sort of mental breakdown.'

'He never says very much,' Nola said. 'Keeps to himself. He's sort of the town ghost. Days go by without anyone seeing him.'

Next, Nola and Monica told me about Sybil Bard, relating the same story about Stewart's death.

Kim spoke up. 'Who else lives here?'

'Well,' Nola snorted. 'There's the big kahuna himself: Ray Pennington. I've never come across a man so full of his own importance.'

'Struts about like a peacock!' Monica agreed.

'Is he married?' I asked.

'He has a wife, Robyn,' Monica said. 'Ray's fifty. Robyn's about forty. She must regret marrying him.'

'He's a big talker,' Nola said. 'About his family. How much property he owns.' She shrugged. 'He's a blowhard. That's all. Then there's Iris Kelly. You'd know her. She owns the general store.'

'It's generally bad,' Monica added, laughing.

'And who else is there?' I asked.

'Well,' Monica continued. 'There's Jamie's parents: Robert and Jean. Both nice people, but work too many hours. Most probably the reason why Jamie went bad. They live next to the general store. Been there about three years. Then there's Karl Hoffman, who lives a few houses down from us.'

'And what's he like?' I asked.

'A strange man,' Nola said. 'Very odd. We've seen him going out at night.'

'We think he worships the moon,' Monica said.

'He could be a werewolf.'

'Don't be silly! Werewolves aren't real!'

'What would you know?'

'Have you ever seen one?'

'No, but that doesn't mean—'

It was hard to believe that a fight was about to break out between them over the existence of werewolves. 'And the other houses around here?' I interrupted. 'The shacks?'

'Empty. Ray's bought a few of them but does nothing with them.' Monica said.

'It's hard to do anything,' Nola added. 'The council doesn't like to approve new building applications because of the ground. At the rate we're going, there'll soon only be us old girls left.'

'Let's hope it doesn't come to that.' I had to speak to every person in town, which would take time. 'Kim and I need to find somewhere to stay—'

'You must stay with us!' Monica said.

'It'll be fun!' Nola added.

I gave a nervous laugh. 'That's a very kind offer,' I said, knowing we would likely go stark raving insane after the first day. 'But we don't want to impose.'

'It's no imposition,' Nola said. 'You can stay in Barbara's room.'

'Who's Barbara?' Monica asked.

'Our great-niece!'

'Her name's Jenny.'

'Did she change it?'

'Of course not! She's always been Jenny!' Monica turned to us. 'Come and look.'

We followed them down to the basement, which someone had transformed into a studio. Unlike the rest of the place, it had only a few pieces of furniture and no knickknacks. It was surprisingly spacious.

This is quite liveable, I thought.

'Jenny's a marine biologist,' Monica said. 'She stays here whenever she comes down here to dive.'

I glanced at Kim, who gave a tiny shrug.

'As long as it's no imposition,' Kim said. 'We don't want to get in the way.'

'You won't get in the way,' Monica said. 'It'll be good to have some company. Nola's a bit batty these days, so—'

'I'm batty?' Nola snapped. 'You're the batty one!'

'At least I know our niece's name—'

I glanced around the room as the twins continued to argue. It had everything we needed. Staying with Nola and Monica would help us gain people's confidence and give us a base to work from. Cape Carson was only twenty minutes from here. Kim and I could still come and go as needed.

'This will be perfect,' I said. 'Thank you so much.'

'It's no problem,' Monica said. 'You girls are mystery fans like us. Having young people staying makes us feel young too.'

Kim and I drove back along Millicent Drive to Cape Carson. It had been a long day already, and it wasn't over yet. We both had to pack a few belongings for our stay in Port Logan. I also wanted to type up my notes from everything Monica and Nola had told us.

It was as we passed the Cape Carson Lighthouse that my phone rang. I hit the speaker button.

'Hey Rosie,' Harry said. 'You anywhere near the boatshed?'

'Just coming back into town now.'

'Good. Can you head down there? Someone rang and said there's a protest going on. Make certain you get some pictures.'

'I've got Kim with me,' I said. 'She can take some pictures too, if you like.'

Harry was momentarily silent. 'Hello Kim,' he said. 'How's that photography coming along?'

He'd seen some of Kim's pictures. Considering she had one of the most modern phones on the market, she still managed to take terrible shots. One day she'd somehow left her phone on and took three hundred pictures of the inside of her handbag.

'I'm improving all the time,' Kim assured him. 'You'll be hiring me full-time as the paper's official photographer soon.'

'I'm sure,' Harry said. 'And pigs might fly.'

I told Harry we'd head down to the boatshed. A few minutes later, we were pulling into the foreshore carpark. The boatshed was an unassuming building nestled under some trees near the wharf. It had been shut for years. Once owned by the council, it had slowly fallen into disrepair. When Giuseppe Costa had purchased it, people had thought he might patch it up and reopen it as a fish and chip shop. It turned out his plans were nothing of the sort.

It was mid-afternoon by now. A dozen people were standing outside the boatshed holding makeshift placards. We got out of my jeep.

'Goodness,' I said. 'That certainly escalated fast. I wonder who's behind this.'

'Possibly some rebellious...person,' Kim said.

There was something odd in her voice. 'Kim,' I said, turning to her. 'What are you saying?'

'Nothing,' she said innocently. 'Some people came into the library to photocopy flyers.'

'And?'

Kim shrugged.

I didn't know what was going on, but I was sure I'd find out soon enough. We headed over to the boatshed where Trixie quickly reacquainted herself with another local dog. The main roller door facing the bay was up too and people were inside. *Maybe they broke in. This could turn into quite a protest.* Most of the people, I knew, if not by name, then by sight.

People sat about on crates, eating food and talking. This was half protest and half party. My eyes scanned the group and I spotted a familiar face, a young waif-like girl named Tilly. She was attractive with dark hair and eyes, and Sandy's partner from the diner. Like her girlfriend, Tilly loved riding Harley-Davidson motorcycles.

'Hey Rosie,' she said warmly. 'You joining us?'

'Just reporting the news,' I said tactfully. 'Are you in charge?'

'No one's in charge.'

The voice from the corner was one I recognised all too well.

'Nan?'

My grandmother sat at a makeshift desk with a half-made sign in front of her. She wore what appeared to be a hastily screen-printed t-shirt that read *Save the Boatshed.*

'You were expecting the Queen of England?' she said. 'Of course, I'm here. Where else would I be?'

Sighing, I settled onto a timber crate opposite her. 'You know that everyone here is breaking the law? You're all trespassing.'

'Sometimes, you need peaceful civil disobedience to get your point across.'

'What does Dave think about this?'

Nan sniffed and pursed her lips. 'Don't mention Dave to me.'

'So he's not on board?'

'We've had a small argument. He thinks I should be doing other things like knitting or watching the days tick over till I die.'

'I'm sure he didn't say that.'

'Not in so many words,' Nan admitted. 'He did say this could be dangerous, and I might get hurt.'

'He could be right.'

'I promised him if the cops stormed the building with truncheons raised that I'd run in the opposite direction.'

The prospect of Todd and his team storming the building with truncheons raised, lowered, or in any other position was pretty much non-existent. More likely, the cops would pop in for a cup of tea and politely ask them to leave.

I got up, took my phone out and grabbed a few pictures as Tilly wandered over.

'Your Nan is amazing,' she said. 'A force of nature.'

'What does Giuseppe Costa make of all this?' I asked. 'He can't be too happy.'

'He's not,' Tilly said. 'Actually, he's threatened legal action. Fortunately, we have a lawyer of our own.' Nodding to a silver-haired gentleman in the corner, she continued, 'Bruce

Ruck is semiretired, but he's happy to represent anyone if we end up in court.'

'Do you think it'll go that far?'

'I'm not sure.'

I asked Tilly a few more questions about the protest and what they hoped to accomplish.

They wanted to have the redevelopment decision over-turned on heritage grounds at this week's council meeting. I glanced across at the people milling about the place. There had never been much interest in the old boatshed. It had just sat here for years. Now it was a hive of activity. Made me think it should have been transformed into something a long time ago. Maybe a café or ice cream place.

My eyes settled on a man in the doorway.

Now, where do I know him from...?

Ah-ha!

I excused myself and crossed to him. 'Hello Keith,' I said. 'Don't tell me you're part of this ragtag crowd. You've only been in town five minutes.'

Keith smiled. 'I'm a sucker for good causes,' he said. 'Seems the town's pretty fired up about saving this place.'

'We're a rebellious bunch.'

'I thought that the first time I met you.'

His green eyes sparkled at me, and I felt that same hot/cold sensation I'd felt earlier. I tried to not let myself get consumed by it. I was a grown woman, after all. My body didn't control my decisions.

At least, I didn't think it did.

'So you're hanging around for a few days?' I asked.

'I suppose so. My mum died a few months back, and I'm sorting out her estate.'

'I'm sorry to hear about your mum. What was her name?'

'Marjorie Allan.' He paused. 'I don't know the town too well. Maybe you could show me around while I'm here?'

Before I could respond, there was movement in the doorway as a bulky figure appeared: Todd. With him was Constable Turner. Todd gave everyone a friendly smile, taking in the sea of faces before focusing on me. He arrowed over.

'Hey Rosie,' he said. 'You in charge of all this?'

'Don't be silly. I'm reporting it.'

'Hmm.'

His eyes crossed to Keith, and I introduced them. At the same time, I noticed Jim Turner saunter over to Samantha, a girl who worked at the Cape Carson Bakery on the weekends. She was a goth girl who was also part of his gaming group. He listened to her as she told him how important it was to fight Giuseppe Costa.

'Looks like you may have already lost your backup,' Keith said, raising an eyebrow.

Todd fixed him with a stare. 'Constable Turner's building

community relations,' he said, glancing about. 'Now here's trouble.'

Of course, the trouble in question was Nan, who headed over to tell him why the boatshed had to be saved.

Todd listened politely until she finished speaking. 'That all sounds wonderful, Nan,' he said. 'But you're still trespassing.'

'And we're going to keep trespassing until the boatshed is saved.'

Todd sighed. 'Can you at least promise that there'll be no damage to property?'

'We're not the ones wanting to demolish this place,' Nan said firmly, turning to everyone. 'Listen up! No damage is to happen to this building! Is everyone clear on that?'

There was a general chorus of agreement.

'You see,' she said, turning back to Todd. 'We're interested in saving the heritage of Cape Carson—unlike some.'

Todd bit his lip. 'The council vote's this week?'

Nan nodded.

'All right,' he said. 'If you can promise that everyone stays peaceful, and no damage will be done to place or person—'

Nan crossed her heart. 'I promise.'

'All right. Although I won't push the issue now, it might be different next time. The law's the law and push might come to shove.'

My grandmother stuck out her chin. 'So be it.'

Todd nodded thoughtfully before separating Jim Turner from Samantha. The forlorn look on the constable's face was something to behold.

Jim was a friendly enough soul and completely unlike Samantha in every way.

Well, I thought. *They say opposites attract.*

I glanced around. Somehow, I'd momentarily forgotten Keith was standing beside me. He was so close that we could have hugged. Raising an eyebrow, Keith gave a small smile. 'Looks like the protesters have won,' he said.

'Yes,' I said, doubtfully. 'But tomorrow's another day.'

His eyes met mine. 'Do you mind if I get your number?'

I tried to remain cool. 'Sure,' I said. 'Mind if I have yours?'

He produced a white business card. 'Call me,' he said. 'Anytime.'

5

'Thanks for agreeing to speak with us,' I said.

Kim and I were sitting in the home of Grace Vickery. It was a nice place, one of the modern steel and glass homes on the west side of Port Logan. This was one of the few places that the council had given approval to build.

The main living room windows looked out onto the bay, West Head and the ocean beyond. A sailing boat edged past at a distance. A flock of seagulls landed on a nearby rock platform. Water came splashing up in great bursts and crashed against the headland.

Trixie, sitting patiently at our feet, yawned.

Grace was about thirty-five with flowing blonde hair, a pointed chin, and blue eyes that seemed too small for her face. She obviously had a taste for antique furniture. Most of the pieces were made from mahogany and rosewood. A few well-chosen ornaments, including a ceramic mouse, decorated a nearby sideboard.

Nan would love something like that, I thought. One of her many hobbies was collecting ceramic mice. Probably Monica and Nola would love one too. A photo of a young woman sat on a window sill. The woman was writing an equation on a blackboard, chalk grasped in her left hand.

'That's my sister Karen,' Grace said. 'She was a school teacher.'

I didn't say anything. Monica had said she died several years ago.

Grace averted her gaze. 'I'm not sure how much I can tell you about the history of the town,' she said. 'I've only lived here about ten years.'

Kim spoke up. 'We're keen to get your impressions of Port Logan. What you think of it, and how you came to be here.'

Grace nodded. 'All right,' she said, gazing through the window at the shifting water in the bay. 'I don't know if I want you publishing this—in fact, I'm sure I don't—but it was a tragedy that brought me here.'

I nodded.

'I grew up in a town called Coopertell in West Australia,' Grace continued. 'There wasn't a lot of money in our family. I suppose you could say we were poor. Our parents died of natural causes, one after the other. Cancer for both of them. Some people thought it may have been because of chemicals they used on their farm.

'Anyway, I fell in love with a guy named Adam. He was very wealthy. Owned a big property. Ten thousand acres. We'd only been married a couple of years when he was killed in a tractor accident. It was a horrible shock. I was devastated, as you can imagine. To get away from it all, my sister Karen suggested I sell up, and we travel for a while. We decided to do a road trip around Australia.

'We were driving through South Gippsland when we stopped at a caravan park where there was a small lake. We took a boat out fishing. In retrospect, it was a terrible idea. Neither of us were good swimmers. I was worse than her. Karen caught a fish. She stood up to reel it in, and the boat tipped over. I tried to save her, but there was nothing I could do.'

'I'm so sorry to hear that,' I said.

'It must have been awful,' Kim added.

'My sister was my world,' Grace said. 'We were inseparable. I didn't want to return to Coopertell. Not after that. I wanted a new life, so I bought the house here.'

'Someone told us you also had a friend who was killed in a hit and run?' I said.

Grace nodded. 'Florence Teale. She'd been a neighbour of ours back in Coopertell. I'd occasionally speak to her on the phone. I invited Florence to come and visit. She'd flown into Melbourne and caught the bus from there. I was going to meet her at the bus stop. You know it arrives here quite late in the evening. I should have been there to meet her, except it turns out we had a mix-up with the dates. I thought she was turning up the next day. It looks like Florence started walking from the bus stop at the top of the hill. That's where she got hit. They never caught the driver. He...'

Grace's voice caught, and her chin quivered.

'Our dear, lovely neighbour came all that way,' she continued. 'Only to die just a few minutes away. I can't believe it's bad luck.' She stopped. 'I'm not saying it has anything to do with the monster either. I don't believe in stuff like that.'

'Grace.' I gave Kim a sideways glance. 'You don't believe that someone wanted to kill Florence deliberately?'

The woman didn't answer immediately. 'I don't want to sound like a crazy person,' she said. 'But I've always suspected that she was run over on purpose.'

'You mean...'

She levelled her gaze at us. 'The driver wanted to kill someone. It made no difference that she was a defenceless old lady. Someone murdered her for the sport of it.'

Kim asked. 'Do you suspect anyone in particular?'

Grace pursed her lips. 'No,' she said. 'Not really.'

It was obvious she wasn't telling the truth.

I said: 'If there's someone you think is responsible—'

'I don't intend to spread rumours,' Grace said. 'Far too much of that happens in Port Logan. I have no idea who could be involved.'

She seemed determined to remain tightlipped.

Fortunately, Kim intervened. 'This is such a beautiful house,' she said, glancing about. 'You must have the best views in town.'

'It's particularly good from the upstairs library. I'll show you.'

Kim and I trailed up the stairs after her. There were paintings on the walls and more antiques. It was obvious Grace loved art and surrounding herself with beautiful pieces. We entered the library, where a picture window looked directly out onto the water. From this view, the derelict houses weren't as noticeable, and it would have been easy to believe that Port Logan was just another beautiful spot on the coast.

Considering she called it the library, it had little in the way of books. Most of the books that were up here were romance novels and old paperbacks. One wall was covered with framed photos. One showed two similar-looking women, Grace and her sister, Karen, when they were younger. The only difference was that one had long hair while the other's was short.

Another picture was of Grace on her wedding day. Her husband leaned over her shoulder, a broad smile on his face as she signed the marriage register with her right hand. He was a handsome man with a square, rugged jaw.

'That's me and Adam at our wedding,' Grace said, her voice

catching. 'Happiest day of my life.'

'You never thought about going back?' I asked.

'No. You can't go back. And I'm used to Port Logan now. Most of the people are pleasant, although there's one disagreeable person—'

At that moment, a figure appeared on the path below. He was short, suntanned, and carrying a timber case.

A frown furrowed Grace's brow.

'Who's that?' I asked.

The woman looked like she wasn't going to answer. 'Ray Pennington,' she said, finally. 'The kingpin of Port Logan.'

6

'Are we in a hurry for any particular reason?' Kim asked as we reached the path.

'Did you see the look on Grace's face when she saw Ray Pennington?'

'That look of dislike?'

'Hate, more like it,' I said. 'He might even be the person she thinks is responsible for her friend's death. And if Ray's responsible for one death—'

'Then he could be responsible for others?' Kim replied.

I didn't answer. We hurried down to the path with Trixie in tow. There was no sign of Ray Pennington. Then we came around a sudden turn and were face to face with him.

Pennington was short, only a little taller than Kim, and stocky. His hair had gone prematurely grey, and his face was deeply tanned. He wore a Hawaiian shirt. He was handsome, although his mouth had an arrogant cast. Now we were closer, I could see the timber case more closely. It was a painter's case with an easel attached. A smear of blue paint ran across the back of one hand.

He nodded. 'Morning.'

'Ray Pennington?' I asked.

'Who wants to know?'

Smiling pleasantly, I introduced us and said we were doing a story on the town. 'We'd love to know what it's like living here,' I said.

'I don't do interviews,' Ray snorted. 'The Cape Carson Gazette has never been kind to Port Logan.'

He was going to be a tough nut to crack. 'I know what you mean,' I said. 'I want to change that. This is a fantastic spot, and I'd like to share that with people.'

Ray seemed taken aback. 'You do?'

'Are you a painter?' Kim asked, peering down at the case.

'I do oil paintings.'

He eased the case open to show us what he'd been working on. As painters go, he was no Leonardo da Vinci. He'd been painting one of the old shacks on the other side of the bay. The painting had a slightly childlike quality to it.

'Goodness,' I said. 'That's amazing.'

Kim did her best to sound enthusiastic. 'Yes,' she echoed. 'Amazing.'

'I've done a few others,' Ray said, brightening. 'Might even have an exhibition one day.'

'I could do a story about your art,' I said. 'When you're ready.'

He closed his case. 'You girls should come back to my place and meet Robyn,' he said. 'She can rustle up a coffee, and I'll tell you about my painting.'

'And your family history,' I prompted. 'I believe your family has been in this area a long time.'

'Since the beginning!' he said grandly. 'We were the first!'

As a matter of fact, the first people here were the aboriginals who inhabited this whole region for thousands of years, but I let it slide. I needed to keep him talking.

His home was the palatial building beside Grace's place, a similar glass and steel structure, with clumps of hydrangeas and gerberas growing along both sides. The walk up the drive was steep, and I silently noted the BMW parked in the garage.

Ray opened the front door. 'Get your gear on, Robyn!' he called with a throaty laugh. 'We've got visitors!'

Great, I thought. *Sounds like we're in for a ball.*

I'd known Ray Pennington for all of two minutes, and I already didn't like him. We went down a short hallway with Trixie close behind and entered a living room that was big and spacious. In fact, everything about the place seemed huge. The lounge chairs were so big they could have easily fit two people, and the television could have shown movies at a Saturday night drive-in.

And yet, for all its palatial aspect, there was something sterile about it.

There's nothing homely about it at all.

The only thing to brighten it up were the artworks on the walls. These were all Ray's original art pieces—and ghastly.

Oh, dear.

There weren't many of them—thank goodness—but the colours seemed all wrong, and they were out of kilter. One was of the section of path where Stewart Bard was killed. Painted before his death, the path angled up in the wrong direction.

'Goodness,' Kim said.

I nodded.

Goodness.

A woman appeared from the kitchen.

This, presumably, was Robyn, a forty-something-year-old woman of Asian appearance. My first impression of her was one of ugliness. I rarely thought that about people, and it took me a moment to reassess my opinion. No, she wasn't ugly. Just someone who rarely smiled. She had dark, wavy hair parted to one side and a tight mouth.

'What a surprise,' Robyn said in perfect English. 'You've brought guests.'

'They're journalists with the paper,' Ray said. 'They want to do a story about our trailblazing family. And my art. Throw on a cuppa, will you luv?'

Robyn ignored him. It was as if he hadn't even spoken. 'I heard we had reporters in town,' she said. 'Iris Kelly said you were asking about Stewart's death.'

Ray's brow creased, and I immediately sought to set it straight again. 'Iris mentioned it,' I said. 'Sounds like a terrible accident.'

'It's the coastline along here,' Ray said, his gaze steady. 'Some of the headlands are limestone and prone to corrosion. People have been told a thousand times to be careful on the paths, especially after rain. They don't listen.'

He asked his wife again to make coffee.

She lingered momentarily, still not looking at him, before disappearing into the kitchen. Ray waved us into seats and began to tell us the history of his pioneering family in Australia. It didn't take long for me to work out that he didn't think anyone else had contributed along the way.

From the time his many-great grandfather had arrived on the First Fleet as a convict, it sounded as if his family had been involved in every major event in the nation's history. And then some.

'We even had a Pennington designing the Sydney Opera House,' Ray continued. 'Helped out on all the difficult bits.'

This was news to me as I'd always thought that a Danish architect named Jørn Utzon had designed the building.

'Goodness,' I said.

'Wow,' Kim added.

Robyn silently appeared, deposited a tray laden with coffee onto the table, and glided from the room as quietly as a ghost. I had the sense that she did that a lot. It was hard to believe that she was Ray's wife and not the maid.

I poured coffee for Kim and myself. Although it was bitter, I didn't mind. It was caffeine, and I needed something to keep me awake while Ray delivered his fantastic history of Australia. My eyes settled on the metal tray. Incredibly, Ray's face had been etched into the surface along with his date of birth.

Good grief!

'...always kept myself fit,' Ray said as he ignored us and poured himself a cup of coffee. 'I'm in the home gym every day. Had an uncle who lived to a hundred and seven...'

'Ray,' I interrupted. 'What you said about the cliffs being limestone was interesting. Is that why the boulder dislodged?'

'What? The boulder? Accidents happen. It's like Cynthia Shepherd.' His eyes narrowed. 'People haven't been telling tales out of turn? Have they?'

I looked at him innocently. 'Oh? You mean about Cynthia?' I said. 'Someone told me she had an accident on her boat. She fell over. Is that true?'

'She only had herself to blame,' Ray said. 'The weather can be rough here, especially in the bay. Her little boat had a big name: *Great Expectations*. Didn't do her much good. During a storm, she went onto her boat to do some work and fell over.'

'I see.' I didn't want to push him, but I had to keep moving forward. 'That seems like an odd accident. She fell on her knife, didn't she?'

'You think someone killed her on purpose?'

I shot the question back at him. 'What do you think?'

'A lot of people didn't like her.'

That was possibly the pot calling the kettle black.

'She rubbed me the wrong way,' Ray continued. 'Said downright nasty things about my paintings and challenged my family history.' He paused. 'I suppose bad things happen to bad people.'

What kind of bad things? I wondered. *Do they get murdered and their deaths made to look like accidents?*

'Other people didn't like her much?' I asked.

Ray grinned unpleasantly. 'Some people liked her too much.'

'You mean…'

'Doctor Taylor—if he ever was a doctor—had a thing for Cynthia. I don't know why. She was old enough to be his mother.'

A scenario started to form in my mind. Sybil said Jamie broke into Philip Taylor's home, stole some alcohol, mixed it with drugs, and died. If Philip had romantic inclinations for Cynthia and was rejected by her, he may have reacted badly.

He might have also had run-ins with other people in town.

Kim seemed to be having the same thoughts.

'You know he's an archaeologist?' she said.

Ray shrugged. 'I haven't seen his credentials.'

'There were also some other deaths.' I tried to sound vague. 'A woman who was run over? One of Grace's friends?'

'That was bad luck,' Ray said. 'I did a painting on that section of road a few years back. One of my first. It's a blind crest as you come over the top. Sometimes we get joyriding kids who come through. I call the cops, but nothing ever happens. I don't know why we pay taxes. The kids stole a car and came roaring down the hill and up the other side into the dunes. It's like a roller coaster for them. That poor lady never had a chance.'

'I hear the car was found burnt out? They never caught the driver?'

'Gives this town a bad name.' He stopped. 'That's why we should have our own council. I'd be a shoo-in as mayor...'

I nodded, but I'd stopped listening as there'd been movement in the doorway. Robyn had paused there, watching silently before disappearing from view. I asked to use the bathroom, leaving Kim to listen to Ray's political ambitions.

Robyn was rinsing plates to stack in the dishwasher. The kitchen was big enough to service a restaurant.

'Ray's on a roll,' she said, without looking at me. 'He loves an audience.'

'Sounds like his family's been in Port Logan a long time.'

'Forever—if you believe him.'

There was no mistaking the bitterness in her voice. 'This town is quite a community,' I said.

'That's one way of putting it.' Robyn wiped her hands and turned to me. 'Anyone who survives here deserves a medal.'

'You don't like it?'

Robyn sighed. 'Ray's got a talent for getting people offside,' she said. 'I heard him mention Cynthia Shepherd. He said people didn't like her? That's not true. *Ray* didn't like her. He wanted to buy a property, and they got into a bidding war over it. He bought it in the end, but it cost double what he wanted to pay.'

'Why did he want to own it?'

'Because he could.'

I nodded without speaking. I was a complete stranger here. If she were telling me this, I wondered what she told other people in Port Logan. 'Someone mentioned they didn't think Cynthia's accident was an accident,' I said, pausing. 'What do you think?'

Robyn started for the door, turning back as she reached it. 'There's something rotten in Port Logan,' she said. 'Something evil. I think it's the monster.'

'Have you seen it?'

'Once.' She hesitated. 'There was a shape in the waters off West Head. A dark thing just below the surface.'

'It could have just been a whale or maybe a seal?'

'No. It was different.' She fixed her gaze on me. 'Maybe the creature has some kind of power. Or this town is cursed. Either way, you should leave while you can. Port Logan isn't safe.'

7

I seem to be here more and more of late, I thought.

'Florence Teale?' Todd said, sitting back from his desk. 'Where do I know that name?'

'She was killed in a hit and run in Port Logan?'

I slipped Trixie a doggy snack.

Todd slowly nodded. 'That's right. I looked her up earlier.' He saw my raised eyebrow. 'You got me thinking about the death of Stewart Bard, and it made me wonder what else has been happening over there.'

'So you know that Florence was the first unusual death.'

'Her death is an ongoing investigation,' Todd said. 'I don't see a link between it and Stewart Bard.'

I let that slide for the moment. I wasn't sure there was a link either, but I was prepared to keep an open mind. 'Can you tell me about the accident?'

Todd brought up the details on his screen. 'Okay,' he said. 'She had travelled from Coopertell in Western Australia to visit a friend living in Port Logan.'

'Grace Vickery.'

'That's right. When Florence arrived, she disembarked the bus from Melbourne at the top of the hill. She'd only just started down Oxley street when she was struck by a vehicle heading west, causing serious head injuries. The coroner said death would have been virtually instantaneous.'

'Did anyone see the accident?'

'Unfortunately, not. Out that way, they're used to hearing hoons up on the main road. One resident reported hearing a thud around six-thirty. That tallies with the arrival time of the bus.'

'Who was that?'

'Iris Kelly.'

'She owns the local shop.'

Todd nodded. 'The woman also said she noticed a vehicle come down the hill soon after,' he said. 'She didn't connect it with the sound of the thud and didn't notice who was driving. Only that it didn't belong to any of the locals. About an hour later, a call came in about a fire in the dunes to the west of town. A patrol car went to investigate and found a vehicle fully alight. First on scene assumed it was simply a joy ride that had ended in a dumped car.

'It wasn't until Florence Teale's body was found that a link was made between the two incidents. The car's front left bumper was damaged. That must have been from when it hit the woman.'

'Her body wasn't found immediately?'

'The impact had thrown her clear off the road and into the undergrowth. It was the investigating officer who made the discovery.'

'Could anything be gleaned from the car?' I asked, but I already knew the answer.

'DNA and fingerprints? No. Sadly, fire's good at destroying evidence. We weren't able to lift anything from the vehicle. The car had been stolen from the library car park.'

I frowned. 'Did it belong to one of the librarians?'

Todd consulted his computer. 'Yes. A girl named Hattie Kale.'

She was one of the younger librarians at Cape Carson. I made a mental note to speak with her about her stolen car. 'So someone stole her car, took it for a joyride, and ran over Florence Teale.'

'That's pretty much it, except...' Todd consulted his screen. 'There's an interesting note here from the attending officer. There was no evidence the car had been broken into. That's unusual.'

I tried to understand what he was saying. 'So, how did they steal the car?'

'It looks like they had a key.'

How was that even possible? I knew Hattie Kale slightly. She was a nice girl. Certainly not the type who would be involved in murder or hit and run accidents. How would they get a key to her vehicle?

Hattie and I would definitely be having a chat.

'What about the other deaths in Port Logan?' I asked.

Todd sat back. 'By the other deaths, you mean…'

I started counting on my fingers. 'Cynthia Shepherd. She fell over on her boat, landed on her knife, and died. Then there's Jamie Farrell, the local delinquent teenager who died of a drug overdose.'

'Rosie,' Todd said. 'You're not saying you think the monster is responsible? Because they sound like accidents or death by misadventure.'

I leaned forward. 'Yes,' I said. 'But what if they're not? What if there's a serial killer in Port Logan?'

'O-kay.'

'Sergeant Todd Parker, wipe that smirk off your face.'

'I'm not smirking. Am I?'

He *was* smirking, which annoyed me, so I stabbed a finger at him. 'Someone could have murdered all those people.'

'And, other than Florence Teale, made their deaths look like accidents?'

'Yes!'

'Possible, Rosie, but not likely. Serial killers usually target a particular victim, and they use the same methodology. That doesn't apply here.'

'Can you at least look into those deaths?'

'I have looked into those deaths.'

That stopped me. 'You have?'

'I do listen to you, Rosie,' he said patiently. 'You are my favourite reporter.'

The way he said it made me want to stare into his eyes. It produced one of those tingling sensations that made me think about spending Saturday night strolling hand-in-hand along the beach with him.

'So,' I said, finding my voice, 'what have you discovered?'

'Only that there's no connection between the deaths,' he said. 'Sure. They all took place in Port Logan. I'll grant you that. But they're all accidents or poor judgment. An elderly woman fell over on her boat and landed on her knife. A kid took drugs. A boulder landed on someone.'

'Or they've been made to look that way.'

'Or they are exactly what they appear to be: unrelated tragic incidents.' He paused. 'It's possible to have statistical clusters. Like lottery wins or house fires, deaths sometimes happen in one area. There's no specific reason for it. Chance just dictates it that way.'

Sighing, I stood up. 'Yep, but I think something more is happening here.'

'And we need evidence,' he said. 'As usual.'

Thanking him, I headed out with Trixie at my heel. Reaching the street, I took a deep breath. Todd was right in saying all these incidents could be chance—but I doubted it. Someone had sent me that note with good reason.

Marching resolutely through town, I reached the Cape Carson Public Library within minutes. Leaving Trixie outside, I headed in to find Kim at the front desk.

'Are we meeting up and I forgot?' she asked. 'Or are you borrowing a book?'

'Neither.' I quickly explained the purpose of my visit. 'Is Hattie around?'

'Reshelving books in the kid's section.'

I found the young librarian buried amongst the children's picture books. Hattie had a big head of red hair, blue eyes and an engaging smile.

'Hattie!' I said. 'You got a moment?'

'Sure.'

After explaining that I was writing about Port Logan, I said I'd heard about her car being stolen and used in a hit and run.

'That was really weird,' she said. 'The police told me that someone had driven the car without breaking in.'

'What does that mean—exactly?'

'They used my car key.' She leaned against the shelf. 'I lost a set of keys from my handbag about a week before. Although it was a nuisance, I didn't think much about it. I assumed they'd fallen out of my bag. Fortunately, I had copies at my mum's place.'

'And later your car was stolen?'

Hattie nodded. 'The police originally thought I committed the hit and run,' she said. 'They only believed me when they discovered I was working that night.'

I thought. 'There's no security cameras in the library?'

'Only on the front door. Unfortunately, the memory drive is overwritten every three days.'

It made sense. After all, this wasn't a bank. It was a public library.

'You didn't see anyone odd on the day your keys went missing?'

Hattie smiled. 'This is a library,' she said. 'There's always somebody strange here. Libraries are one of the few public places where you can hang out for free. There's a couple of homeless people who come in each day as well as a few retired people who have nothing much to do.'

'Could your keys have been taken by any of them?'

'I've never had anything stolen before when they were here, and nothing's gone missing since.'

After thanking Hattie, I returned to Kim's office, where she was working on her computer. 'You got a minute?'

'Sure.'

I related what I'd learned.

'So whoever stole the keys wasn't a run-of-the-mill thief,' Kim said. 'And we can't even blame the monster because it doesn't leave Port Logan.'

'The monster clearly doesn't have a driver's licence.'

'Now *you're* being silly.'

I didn't reply to that. 'It sounds like the person who stole the keys may have been planning ahead.'

'And their intention was to use the car to kill someone? That's terrible.'

I thought about the other deaths. 'This could mean that all those deaths are random murders by one person,' I said. 'They're some kind of...thrill kills, I suppose you'd call it. The killer sets out to murder someone. Maybe they don't even care who it is.'

'What did Todd say?'

'He practically laughed me out of his office when I said a serial killer could be at large.' I thought about Nola, Monica and all the other people living in Port Logan. 'No. We've got to solve this ourselves. Everyone in Port Logan is in danger. There's a killer targeting that area—and we've got to find them!'

8

'Giuseppe,' I began crisply. 'Can you tell me your views about the protesters at the boatshed?'

As well as interviewing the residents around Port Logan, I also needed to pursue the story about the boatshed. A call to Giuseppe Costa's office had resulted in a meeting with the property developer.

I glanced out the window. Giuseppe's office had a grand view of Cape Carson beach, all the way from Cut Rock Lookout at one end to the lighthouse at the other. The developer sat, turning over a paperweight in his hand. He was proud of that paperweight. The clear Perspex object contained the first twenty dollars he ever earned.

'Is this on the record?' he asked.

'Uh, yes.'

'Shame.' He barked a short laugh and sat the paperweight down with a clunk. Giuseppe was a short man with a bad combover and eerily reminiscent of the actor, Danny de Vito.

'There are many things I could say off the record. Those kinds of things you can't publish in the paper.'

'Giuseppe's a patient man.' His wife, Sharon Costa, sat on the sofa behind me. She was a tall blonde with a prominent nose. 'He gets upset when people rub him the wrong way.'

'Is that how you feel about things?' I asked, turning back to Giuseppe. 'Upset?'

He spread his arms. 'What people don't understand is that I own that boatshed,' he said. 'I can do whatever I want with it. I can renovate it. Drive a bulldozer through it. Throw up a twenty-storey building if I want.'

'Council regulations wouldn't allow—'

'If I want to turn it into a waste dump or build a nuclear reactor, I can do that,' Giuseppe interrupted me. 'It's *my* land. *My* land. I don't know how much clearer I can be about that. That property went up for sale, and I bought it. Other people had the option, and they didn't do the same.'

Sharon cut in. 'They probably didn't have the money, luv.'

'Bad luck for them,' Giuseppe said. 'Good luck for me.'

'And what plans do you have for the boatshed?' I asked.

Giuseppe peered into the distance. 'A lovely little building,' he said. 'An icon for the area. It'll be a classy joint...place...that'll serve fish and chips, ice creams, and drinks.'

'A fast food place?'

'Not a dive,' he said. 'Nothing like that. Classy.'

'Tell Rosie what you're calling it,' Sharon prompted.

'Okay, Rosie,' he said. 'Picture this.'

'All right.'

He held out his hands as if visualising the billboard for a major motion picture. 'You'll love this,' he said. '*Giuseppe's*.'

I was momentarily struck dumb. 'Wow,' I said, finally. 'Giuseppe's.'

Trixie yawned.

'In big letters,' Giuseppe added.

Even small letters sounded awful. Actually, the whole idea was so hideous that I momentarily considered joining the protestors. Then I reminded myself that I needed to remain impartial. Maybe a dialogue between the two parties would be interesting?

'Would you be interested in meeting with the protestors?' I asked. 'Having a conversation? Maybe hearing their concerns?'

'Only if they're peaceful,' Sharon spoke up. 'I don't want them lynching Giuseppe. He's the only husband I've got.' She stopped. 'Although, he's got a lot of life insurance.'

I wasn't sure how to take any of that, so I turned to Giuseppe. 'It sounds like they don't know your plans,' I said. 'You might be able to convince them to move on.'

Giuseppe rubbed his chin thoughtfully. 'Some of them

could be misinformed,' he said. 'They might think I'm some kind of greedy developer.'

I let that comment slide.

'I can meet them,' he said. 'When?'

'How about this evening?' I glanced at my watch. 'Six o'clock?'

'Okay,' he said. 'But they'd better be wearing shoes. I've never gotten on with people who don't wear shoes.'

Thanking Giuseppe, I headed from his office with Trixie in tow and drove down to the boatshed. There seemed to be more people than ever at the site.

I noted—with some disappointment—that Keith was nowhere to be seen. Nan was still there, however, as was Ellie with her boyfriend, Ralph, a lanky guy with unkempt blonde hair that fell across his forehead.

'You've been roped into this too?' I asked the pair.

'Places like this have got to be protected,' Ellie said. 'They're part of the area's history.'

Ralph joined in. 'Too many old buildings have already been knocked down in Cape Carson,' he said. 'Once they're gone, they're gone forever.'

Nodding, I headed over to Nan and told her that Giuseppe was coming down to speak to everyone.

'Good,' Nan said. 'We can arrange a horrible accident—'

'Nan!'

'Kidding! Maybe we can reach some kind of agreement. A place in the middle.'

'That's more like it,' I said.

I glanced at my watch. There was still an hour till Giuseppe was meeting the group, so I decided to take a walk. I went for my usual stroll along the coastal path up to the lighthouse. Trixie trotted along ahead of me. As far as she was concerned, any time was a good time for walking. With winter coming on, the sun was already low in the sky, and the water was calm and clear.

A woman came toward me, flashing a smile.

Who is—?

Then I remembered: Sadie.

'Hello,' I said. Sadie was dressed a little more appropriately than the last time I'd seen her. Actually, she was wearing a similar outfit to me: slacks, a blouse, and a jacket. At her side was a white poodle. Trixie immediately gave her a sniff.

'This is Lady Cha-Cha,' Sadie said.

Both Trixie and Lady Cha-Cha's tails wagged.

'They seem to like each other,' I said.

'They do. Out for a stroll?'

'I often come this way,' I said. 'It's good to clear my head.'

'George was saying you're a journalist. Must be stressful.'

'I don't know if I'd call it stressful,' I said. 'There's always a lot happening.'

She frowned. 'Is there some kind of protest at that boat-shed?'

I explained about Giuseppe Costa wanting to redevelop it. 'He's meeting with the protesters tonight.'

'George said he's a shifty character,' Sadie said. 'Might need to watch yourself. Oh, and you're still okay for dinner?'

'Sure. We'll be there.'

'Great.'

Sadie looked genuinely pleased.

Saying goodnight, she continued down in the direction of town while I made a loop around the lighthouse. By the time I was heading back the same way, she was gone from sight. I was having quite positive thoughts about her, and I wasn't sure why, so I sat down on the nearest bench and gave Kim a call.

'Why don't I hate her?' I asked Kim after explaining my conflicting emotions.

'Why would you? You don't even know the woman.'

'But she's...' My voice trailed away. I'd been about to say that she had broken up my relationship with George, but that wasn't true. She didn't break up our relationship. Blossom and George had done that, and Blossom was no longer on the scene. Sadie was an innocent bystander who had come along years later. 'I suppose you're right. I don't know her.'

'And maybe you're moving on,' Kim suggested. 'You don't have the same feelings for George.'

'That's true,' I said. Trixie put her head on my lap, and I stroked her back. 'It's been years now. He's moved on with his life, and I have too.'

'And you have Todd.'

I did an eye roll. 'Nothing's happening with Todd.'

'Nothing?'

'Nothing much.' Other than a kiss goodnight, our relationship—if it could be called that—was still at square one. 'He's a nice guy, though.'

'You could do worse, and you're doing better than me. I had to get my car fixed the other day.'

'And you took it to Robert?'

'He and Alex are the best in town.'

Her ex and his new partner owned the garage on Hammond Street. 'You're right there,' I told her. 'I took my jeep to Joey Toxten's garage in Phillip Street to change a headlight, and it took him half a day to work out how to remove the cover.'

Kim sighed. 'When am I going to meet a nice guy?'

'When the time's right. He'll take one look at you and realise you're absolutely perfect.'

'You think so?'

'I know it.'

Wishing her goodnight, I hung up and glanced at my watch. It was almost six o'clock. Trixie and I hurried back down the hill and reached the boatshed just as Giuseppe and Sharon arrived. The group was larger than ever; word must have gotten around that they were turning up.

He marched in the door and peered at the assembled crowd. I wondered if he was memorising their faces to enact revenge later. Nan pushed through to the front.

'Giuseppe,' she said. 'We've heard a rumour that you're planning to knock this place down.'

'Nan Ryan.' Giuseppe said her name slowly, shooting me a quick look as if to blame me for having such a cantankerous grandmother. 'It's more than a rumour. I'm getting rid of this eyesore and putting in a nice new place.'

'It's not an eyesore to everyone. This place has got history.'

Giuseppe sighed. 'How old is this building?' he said. 'A hundred years? That's nothing. The Greeks and Italians were building places ten times this size thousands of years ago. Stonehenge is even older. This is an old shed. It's nothing.'

Tilly stepped forward. 'It isn't nothing,' she said. 'This place means something.'

Someone called out from the back of the crowd. 'I kissed my wife behind this shed for the first time!'

'So what?' Giuseppe asked.

'I did more than that with my wife!' another voice called out.

There was a ripple of laughter. A lady lifted her hand. 'My Henry and I sit on the front step and watch the water,' she said.

Another man raised his voice. 'My son and I used to wash and fillet our fish here,' he said. 'He's gone now. Cancer. I still think of him every time I pass this place.'

Giuseppe turned to the group. 'You've got to have progress,' he said. 'This boatshed's been empty for years. It'll employ half a dozen people when it reopens and bring visitors to the water at night. The whole town will benefit.'

'We're not against that,' Nan said. 'But why can't you just fix up what you've got?'

'For the money I'd spend fixing up this place, I could put up a brand new building: better, cleaner, more stylish. You'll like *Giuseppe's* when it's done.'

This was greeted with confused silence.

'*Giuseppe's*?' Nan said. 'That's what you're calling it?'

'What a silly name,' a woman near the front said.

'It's not silly,' Giuseppe said. 'It's my name.'

'But it's always been the Cape Carson Boatshed!' a man declared. 'I proposed to my wife here.'

'You can't change the name!' someone yelled.

'Save the boatshed!' Tilly chanted. 'Save the boatshed!'

A chorus of voices joined her. Even Trixie joined in, howling along with the crowd. Giuseppe tried to make his voice heard, but it was impossible. Muttering something under his breath, he pushed through the crowd with Sharon close behind. I hurried after them into the cold night air.

'What will you do now?' I asked as they climbed into their black Mercedes.

'This isn't over yet,' Giuseppe said.

'The council meeting's tomorrow night,' I said. 'What if they vote against you?'

Giuseppe's face was unreadable in the growing twilight. 'There's more than one way to skin a cat,' he said. 'We'll see what happens.'

9

'Nola and I have been talking,' Monica said.

'About what?' Nola asked.

'Karl! Don't you remember?'

'The man on the morning show?'

'No! Karl Hoffman!'

'Oh—that Karl!'

It was the next day, and Kim and I had spent the night in their basement flat. It had been a comfortable night's sleep, despite my mind being in a whirl about what was happening with the boatshed. The whole episode was coming to a head and I had no idea as to the outcome. I'd woken early and taken Trixie for a walk while Kim got ready. Arriving back, I found that Nola and Monica had made breakfast for us.

Sitting around their breakfast table, the old ladies ladled bacon and eggs onto our plates. One piece of bacon fell on the floor, and Trixie gobbled it up like a seagull after a chip. I wondered what time the old ladies had gotten up.

Or had they never slept? Had they spent the night trawling the streets in a search for blood?

'What is it about Karl Hoffman?' I asked. 'He's one of your neighbours, I believe?'

'We don't like to spread rumours,' Nola said. 'That only causes trouble.'

'Snitches get stitches,' Monica confirmed. 'That's what they say in jail. But you need to know what's been going on.'

'Okay.' I waited. 'What *has* been going on?'

The old ladies leaned in. So did we.

'Karl's argued with just about everyone,' Nola said.

'Even us,' Monica declared. 'He said we were playing Bing Crosby too loudly.'

'No! It was Perry Como!'

'Are you sure?'

'Of course, I'm sure. I don't even like Bing!'

I cut in. 'You're saying Karl can be difficult?'

'He's always been a sourpuss!' Monica said.

'Then I think we need to interview him,' I said to Kim.

She agreed. We got ready and were soon heading down the East side path. The twin's living room looked across to his front porch. Karl's place was one of the worst beach shacks in the area. There was no garden. Only rock, sand, salt bush, and a stubborn Tea-tree. A car with flat tyres lay slumped beside the house. One of the shutters on Karl's place banged repetitively.

A string chime of seashells rattled and sang in the wind.

It was early, but the morning was unseasonably warm. Rain had been threatening for days now, but it was definitely on the way. Bulbous grey clouds were massing on the horizon.

As we approached, furious barking came from inside the house, causing Trixie to prick up her ears. The verandah's timber flooring was covered with strange carvings that had long ago been coloured with red and green paint. The colours were faded, but the tracings remained.

I wonder what they mean.

I banged on the screen door. It was so dusty that I couldn't see beyond.

'Yes?'

It was impossible to make out the figure; all I could see was a biggish form and something that looked like a grey beard. At his feet was a scruffy-looking dog. A terrier cross, by the look of it. I introduced myself and Kim, saying we were putting together an article about the history of the area and the people who lived there.

'Not interested,' the man said.

'It would be helpful to get—'

'No.'

The voice sounded so firm that I was about to give up. Then Kim chimed in.

'Are they conch shells?' Kim asked. 'For good luck?'

I looked to where she pointed to one of the many images engraved into the timber decking. Now I looked more closely. Kim was right. They were overlapping images of conch shells, which was why it had been so difficult to make them out.

'You need good luck around here,' Karl said.

'Because of the monster?'

The screen door creaked open, revealing a heavyset man with unkempt grey hair and a wispy beard. He wore a dusty, short-sleeved chequered shirt, shorts, and a pair of worn sandals. He regarded Kim carefully. 'What do you know about the monster?'

'I saw it once many years ago.'

'Once you see it,' Karl said, 'you can never forget it.'

I nodded to the carvings. 'Did you carve those?'

'I did,' Karl said. 'You need protection against that...thing. And I have my dog, Sirius.' His eyes zigzagged between Kim and me. 'The best advice I can give you is to leave.'

'Can you tell us what you know?'

Sighing, Karl pointed us into the dusty seats at the end of the verandah. He settled down opposite, the little terrier on his lap. It immediately lay down its head to sleep.

'So you've seen the monster?' Kim said.

'I have seen it.'

Kim gave me a look: *See, I told you so!*

'The creature lives in the waters off Port Logan,' Karl said.

'I hear its thoughts.'

Naked fear flashed across the man's face. Trixie went over and placed her head on his knee.

Oh dear, I thought. *This poor man is crazy.*

'There's a lot of sealife off the coast,' I said. 'Dolphins. Whales. Seals—'

'It is the creature,' Karl said, flatly.

Arguing with him seemed pointless. 'Several people have died,' I said. 'The most recent was Stewart Bard.'

Karl nodded. 'Stewart never spoke to me,' he said. 'He kept his distance, although I sometimes saw him in the mornings.'

'And the day he died?'

'I heard the rockfall. The one that killed him. I didn't know what it was. Then Grace was calling for help.'

'You didn't see anyone else on the path?'

'No.'

'What about the other deaths around here?'

'Oh, you mean that teenager?' Karl's face darkened. 'Some people who die deserve it. They displease the creature, and it takes its revenge.'

I suppressed an eye roll. *Good grief.* 'I understand Jamie Farrell was a handful.'

'He poisoned my garden.'

This was news to me. 'Really?'

'I was growing tomatoes behind my house. One day I saw

him spraying something on them. Within a few days, they died.'

That fits with Jamie being a juvenile delinquent, I thought.

'Did you tell Jamie's parents?' Kim asked.

Karl shrugged. 'They were never around—and they would not have listened. I said something to them one day, and they called me a crazy old man.'

I let this pass without comment. 'The day Jamie died,' I said. 'Were you around?'

'I saw him.'

'Was he alone?'

Karl nodded. 'And you're going to ask me about the others too,' he said. 'Cynthia Shepherd. The old woman would stare at me. I did not like it.'

'And Florence?' Kim asked.

'The woman who was run over?' He looked away. 'I know nothing about her.'

'Can you think of anyone who would want to hurt these people?' I asked.

He hesitated. 'No person,' Karl said. 'Only the creature.'

I wondered about Karl. There could be a good reason why he was blaming the creature: to divert attention from himself. Karl could have killed all those people and not even realised it. I watched him pat Trixie's head. It was hard to believe he would do such a thing. He didn't seem mentally capable of stealing a car to run someone over. And how would he force Jamie Farrell to take the drugs?

I gave a slight nod to Kim.

Time to leave.

'We'd better get going,' she said. 'Thanks for your time.'

We got up.

'It is a full moon tonight,' Karl said suddenly. 'It is best to stay at home when the moon is full.'

I didn't bother asking him why.

'I like your dog,' Karl said unexpectedly. 'Keep her close. The monster is dangerous.'

Thanking him again, we headed back down the path, aware that Karl was watching our every step. Kim and I didn't speak again until we were almost back at Nola and Monica's place.

'What do you make of all that?' I asked.

'Well,' Kim said, considering. 'We shouldn't go out tonight.'

'Are you kidding? We have to go out tonight!'

'But Karl said—'

'Kim,' I said, sighing. 'Karl's deranged, but there might be some reason why he doesn't want people wandering about on moonlit nights.'

'Why do you think that is?'

'I have no idea. But he could be the killer.'

'Really?'

I hesitated. 'We can't rule him out,' I said. 'Karl's definitely strange. He might have killed all those people and is projecting the blame on the creature. We need to keep an eye on his place and see what goes on.'

'You take too many risks, Rosie,' Kim grumbled. 'I better not get eaten by anything.'

'The only thing you'll be eaten by is mosquitos. Good thing I packed some spray.'

The day passed quickly. It seemed a good idea to drop by the homes of the people we hadn't interviewed yet, but that produced no results.

Neither Philip Taylor nor Jamie Farrell's parents were home. Nola and Monica told us that wasn't unusual. Both Robert and Jean Farrell worked and were often out. Philip Taylor came and went whenever he pleased.

By the time the afternoon rolled on, I felt a headache coming on. Nola cautioned that it could be a brain tumour.

'Josh Egland was killed by a tumour back in ninety-four,' she said. 'He dropped dead mid-conversation.'

'Thanks,' I said. 'I'll try to finish my sentences quickly.'

I took a few headache pills and lay down. When I awoke next, my hair was plastered against my face, and Kim was reading her phone on her bed. It looked like most of the day had come and gone.

She glanced over. 'You're alive,' she said.

'You had doubts?'

'I did check for a pulse occasionally.' She put her phone down. 'I had a chat with Nola and Monica about Karl.'

'What did they say?'

'Well, they told me all about their arthritis. Although Nola's usually isn't too bad, it plays up on cold mornings. Monica's, on the other hand—'

'Anything about Karl?'

'Only that they've seen him leave his place around nine o'clock on moonlit nights. He apparently heads over to Piper beach.'

That was the beach beyond East Head.

'Really?' I considered this. 'Do they know why?'

'No.' Kim's face fell. 'I suppose we've got to follow him—without getting eaten by the monster.'

'I think we'll be fine.'

Nola and Monica insisted on having us come for dinner. We squeezed in around the cramped kitchen table as they ladled big helpings of stew into bowls. Kim and I tried some.

'Wow,' I said. 'This is delicious.'

'It's lovely,' Kim echoed. 'What's it called?'

'Bitstew,' Nola said.

'Bitstew?' I said. It sounded Eastern European. 'What's in it?'

'A bit of everything,' Nola said. 'That's why we call it

bitstew. We've just been adding whatever we find. Haven't washed the pot since nineteen sixty-seven.'

'I put a lemon in today,' Monica added.

I coughed. 'That explains the kick.'

After dinner, Kim and I got changed into dark clothing and watched Karl's home from our basement window. It wasn't long before we saw his front door ease open and the big man appear. By now, the sun was down, and the moon was bright in the sky, casting its silvery glow across the shimmering water.

Karl looked in both directions before starting for the nearest headland. Leaving Trixie behind, Kim and I silently raced out the door and onto the path. We scurried around the bay in pursuit. Most houses were in darkness, although light and sound seeped from a few. A big-screen television was on at the home of Ray and Robyn Pennington, with a smaller version playing at Grace Vickery's place. A discordant jangle of jazz music emanated from Philip Taylor's house.

We rounded the headland, following the narrow path along the shoreline. A fifty metre drop lay below; above was a steep incline, boulders, and loose scree. I peered nervously up at the ominous rocks lining the crest of the hill above. From up there, a boulder had come crashing down onto Stewart Bard.

We traversed the section of shattered path and took the lower trail around the next headland. There was no sign of Karl. He could be lying in wait around the bend. We nervously followed the path as it angled down to Piper beach. I motioned Kim up into the sand dunes beyond, and we took refuge in a shadowy slipface.

'Can you see him?' I whispered.

Kim said, 'No...wait a moment. Yes!'

A figure emerged from the edge of the beach: Karl. He stopped about ten metres from the water. Producing a stick, he made a circle in the sand with himself at the centre.

'What's he doing?' Kim asked.

'Dancing the rhumba!' I hissed. 'How would I know?'

Karl laid down the stick and raised his arms high into the air. Directly ahead of him lay the ocean and the glistening light of the moon. He seemed to be praying to the lunar body.

He's performing some kind of ceremony.

I was just about to share this with Kim when Karl gripped his shirt and pulled it up over his head.

'Maybe he's going for a swim,' Kim said.

Karl reached down and removed his shorts.

'Or maybe not,' I said.

10

'Georgiana Shepherd?' I said. 'My name's Rosie.'

The woman at the half-open door was in her early forties with black, stringy hair and pasty skin. Everything about her was pudgy, down to the fingers clutching the cigarette in her left hand.

'The reporter?' she said.

'That's me. I rang you this morning. I wanted to speak to you about your mum, Cynthia.'

The adventure Kim and I had undertaken the night before had ended around ten o'clock. After Karl had stripped naked, he had performed a strange ceremony where he did a series of yogic salutes to the moon for about half an hour. All the while, he had recited some strange chant that hadn't been in any tongue I recognised, although I suspected it was Gaelic or Welsh.

At the end of it all, he put his clothes back on and returned to town. Passing by us, his face had been a mixture of rage and then terror and then laughter that broke through the night. My stomach had dropped at the sight. *He's completely mad* was what went through my mind. Of course, that didn't make him a killer. He could be harmless. Either way, he had to remain high on our list of suspects. Kim and I had trailed behind him at a safe distance before returning to Nola and Monica's place.

The lead for Georgiana Shepherd had come from Harry. I'd asked Kim if she were available to come along, but she'd had to work.

'Don't call me Georgiana,' she said. 'My mum named me that. Everyone calls me Georgie.'

'Okay. Can we chat?'

'Is there money in this?' Georgie asked.

'Money?'

'For selling my story.'

'You're not really selling your story,' I said, doing my best to sound upbeat. 'I'm doing a history piece on Port Logan, and I noticed a few people had died there recently.' I added, unnecessarily, 'Your mum was one of them.'

She still seemed undecided. Then Georgie's face angled down to Trixie. 'That your dog?'

It was a dumb question.

No, I just found it wandering the streets and thought I'd bring it along!

'Yes,' I said. 'This is Trixie.'

'I've always loved beagles,' Georgie said.

'Me too.'

'All right,' she said grudgingly. 'Come in.'

Georgie opened the door wide, and I went inside. She lived northwest of Cape Carson in a tiny town called Melhouse. The area had a main street with half a dozen sidestreets lined with fibro and weatherboard homes. Mobs of kangaroos roamed the surrounding paddocks.

Georgie's place was full of old-fashioned furnishings and walls made sepia from smoking. The whole place stunk of cigarettes. My eyes searched for an open window. So did Trixie. She gave a little whine as we entered.

Georgie led me through to the kitchen, where she was drinking a cup of instant coffee. 'Want a coffee?' she asked. 'Or something stronger?'

Being just after eleven o'clock, I definitely didn't want anything stronger.

'Water's fine,' I said.

She poured a cup, and we sat down. 'So you're not here about the monster?' she asked.

'I've heard of it.'

'Everyone's heard of it.'

I took out my pen and pad and started to take notes. 'There's been a few deaths in Port Logan recently.'

'Yeah.' Georgie sat back and leisurely lit another cigarette.

'There was mum and a teenage kid who died. And some guy got squashed by a rock, I think.'

'Your mum owned her home in Port Logan?'

'Yeah?' Her brow creased. 'What of it?'

'I was wondering who inherits now she's gone.'

Georgie didn't answer for a moment as she took a long drag on her cigarette. 'I got half,' she said. 'I've got a brother in Queensland who gets the other half. I want to sell up, but he's not ready.' She blew out the smoke. 'We didn't know mum well.'

I nodded, waiting.

'Mum had been on boats since she was twelve. She'd been a deckhand, kitchen hand, navigator, and captain. Had my brother and me when she was nineteen. Knew it was no life for us and let a cousin raise us. So we never knew her. Not really.'

'Some suspicions have been raised around your mum's death.'

Georgie's eyes narrowed. 'What are you saying? That we did something to mum?'

'Not at all.'

'Because I do think mum was killed.'

'Really?' Now she had my attention. 'Who do you think killed her?'

'Ray Pennington. He and mum fought for years. She hated him as much as he hated her. But the thing about Ray Pennington is that he's got a motive.'

'Which is?'

'He reckons that whole town should belong to him. You know one of his ancestors owned that whole section of coast?'

'Really?'

'That's what Ray says, and he wants it back. It's his legacy. That's what he told mum one day. He wants to get back every last piece of land that his great-great-whatever owned, and he won't be satisfied until everything belongs to him.'

Ray hadn't said any of this to Kim and me. Maybe he knew how it would sound.

Georgie continued, giving me a grin that revealed a thin line of nicotine-stained teeth. 'Ray looks fit,' she said. 'He does all that bodybuilding and goes out on his boat all the time. But you know he had a heart attack three years back? It almost killed him. Maybe we'll be luckier next time.'

No love lost here.

'Your mum supposedly fell over on the boat,' I said.

'Yeah.' The woman laughed harshly. 'A load of rubbish.'

'You don't believe it?'

'Before moving to Port, she'd sailed around the world six times. Survived a typhoon off China's East Coast and a ship-wreck in South America. The idea that she could fall on a knife is a joke. That's what I told the cops, but they ignored me.'

'This was Cape Carson police? Was it Sergeant Wilson?'

'That guy was hopeless. The new guy's probably not much better.'

I didn't want to get into a conversation defending Todd. 'There have been other deaths too,' I said.

'I don't know anything about them.' She stopped. 'Apart from that teenager. I saw him have a run-in with Ray.'

I asked her to tell me about it.

'I was visiting mum,' Georgie said. 'There was some yelling, and we saw the kid on the other side of the bay. Ray was screaming something at him. The kid yelled something rude back. Ray actually chased him. I thought he was going to have another heart attack. No such luck. The kid disappeared up the road and into the dunes.'

'Any idea what was going on?'

'Ray said the kid spray painted the side of his house. I looked later. Some crude stuff was written there.' Georgie grinned. 'Ray was screaming blue murder. Said he was going to kill that kid. If you think someone killed mum and the kid, it was probably Ray.'

I digested all this. Ray had argued with just about everyone in town. He was a control freak and needed to own everything in sight. His temper was legendary, and he'd threatened to kill at least one person.

'Although,' Georgie continued, putting out her cigarette and lighting another. 'It could always be Robyn.'

Huh?

'Robyn?'

'Yeah. His wife. Barely ever spoke to mum when she was alive. On the day of mum's funeral, though, I saw her at the cemetery. She was standing by herself under some trees, watching the service. When it was all over, I went over to speak to her, but she was gone.'

I wonder why she was there.

It could have been to pay her last respects. If that were the case, though, wouldn't it have made more sense to actually attend the funeral? Robyn could have had a motive to kill these people. Maybe something we hadn't discovered yet.

'Was there anyone else from the town at her funeral?' I asked.

'A few. The old ladies were there: Nola and Monica. And Iris, the woman from the shop. Sybil and Stewart. Jean and Robert, although they left their brat son at home. Karl was there, too, even though he's a crazy person.'

'Did your mum have any problems with him?'

'No.'

'Philip Taylor wasn't there?'

She hesitated. 'He couldn't make it.'

'And your brother?'

Georgie glanced at her watch. 'Sorry. Just remembered that I've got to be somewhere. I'd better go.'

I thanked her and returned to my car. I sat in silence for a moment with the engine running. There had been something odd in the way Georgie had abruptly ended the interview. Something about her brother. Maybe they didn't get on. I wished Kim were with me, but she'd still be at work for hours. I missed having her at my side. Her input was valuable.

Trixie gave a loud sigh.

'I know what you mean,' I said.

I drove back to Port Logan. It was midday by the time I arrived, and the town was quiet as I coasted down the hill. Although the door to Iris Kelly's shop was open, there was no one around. The water in the bay gently pushed against the boats. The streets were empty.

What an eerie place.

No wonder Port Logan had such a weird reputation. I pulled into Nola and Monica's driveway and climbed out. Trixie barked excitedly at the sight of the water.

'Feel like a walk?' I said to her. 'Come on, girl. Let's see if we can track down that old monster.'

We took the path past West Head. This led around to Cullen beach. Below the path lay a rock platform with the water crashing over the side. Trixie stopped and stared at the water. She barked.

'What is it, girl?' I asked. 'Is it a seal? Or some fish?'

She stared into the water, took a step back, and barked

again. I followed her gaze, but the glittering sunlight on the water made visibility impossible. Trixie could see something I couldn't. A dark form moved under the surface. *Is that a seal?* Stepping forward to take a closer look, the loose ground slid from under me, and I yelled. Trixie barked frantically as I slid down the dirt hill on my backside.

'Oh—*bum*!' I looked up at Trixie peering down at me from the path. 'Yes,' I told her. 'I've done it again.'

Muttering under my breath, I climbed back to the path. Nothing had been hurt. Only my dignity and my slacks now had a big dirty smear down the back. Just as I was dusting them off, a man appeared from around the next hill.

'All right?' he asked.

The stranger looked about forty, lanky, with black hair combed to one side. He wore thick-lensed glasses, a grey t-shirt, and black jacket.

I wondered if we'd met before. The man seemed vaguely familiar, though it might have been his similarity to a university professor I'd once had.

'I'm fine, thanks.' Inspiration struck me. 'Would you be Doctor Taylor?'

He blinked. 'Technically,' he said, 'it's Professor Taylor. My speciality is archaeology.'

I introduced myself and gave my spiel about the history article. Philip stared at me, his face unreadable.

'I see,' he said, finally. 'I suppose you want to know about the monster.'

'And other things. Have you seen the monster?'

'No,' he said. 'Although others say they've glimpsed it. I neither believe nor disbelieve in its existence.'

'Can we sit somewhere?' I asked. 'I've spoken to everyone else in town. It would be nice to get your perspective, Doctor.'

'Call me Philip. There's a park bench around the other side of the hill.' He glanced back at me. 'Try not to fall off the path.'

'I'll try,' I told him. 'But I can't promise anything.'

If I'd expected a laugh, I didn't get one. He simply grunted. I followed him around the bend. The bench turned out to be further away than I expected. It was hot in the sun and getting hotter by the moment. Fortunately, shading the seat was an ancient tea tree that had survived the relentless onslaught of the onshore winds. Trixie lay flat on the ground to cool her body as we settled down.

Philip started. 'Rosie, you've probably worked out that the rumours are true,' he said. 'We're a dysfunctional lot in Port Logan.'

'I wouldn't say *dysfunctional*.'

'Then you're too polite.'

'You seem to have a high opinion of your neighbours.'

Philip pursed his lips. 'I think very well of some of them. The old dears you're staying with—Nola and Monica—are lovely.

Maybe a bit batty, although that's to be expected at their age.'

So you've noticed us staying with Nola and Monica. Philip obviously kept an eye on the neighbourhood from behind his closed blinds.

He continued. 'Then there's Karl Hoffman. He's friendly enough but nutty as a fruitcake. I believe he was a member of a cult years ago. Or still is. Either way, I'm not sure he should be freely wandering about the streets.

'Then there's Ray and Robyn, the local Kingpin and this wife. Ray is a total megalomaniac. I don't know how Robyn lives with him.

'Next, we've got Grace. Very pleasant, but traumatised by what's happened in her life: the death of her husband, sister, and recently, her friend. She should probably be in therapy.' He rubbed his chin. 'We also have Iris, who runs the corner shop, if you can call it that. Some of the items on her shelves should be in a museum. And last we have Sybil, our grieving widow—or she seems to be.'

'What do you mean *seems to be*?'

'I've visited her garden centre once or twice. That place should have closed years ago. How is it still running? Mind you, with Stewart's death, she may have received a huge insurance payment.'

'Not everyone has life insurance,' I pointed out.

'True. But that was a strange accident, don't you think? A

boulder falls off a cliff and crushes someone who happens to be walking below. You need to ask yourself who profits. In this case, it's her.' An unexpected smile split his face. 'And I've left the best till last: Jean and Robert Farrell. They gave birth to Jamie, known locally as Demonspawn. Full points to whoever killed him off. If it was Ray, then he did us all a service.'

I doubted Jamie's parents would appreciate hearing such sentiments about their son. 'Jamie was only seventeen,' I said.

'And still out of jail,' Philip said. 'That's the biggest surprise of all. He may have been mentally challenged. I don't know. All I know is that he terrorised this town. Everyone's place got graffitied or damaged. The police were rung half a dozen times. Nothing ever happened, of course.'

'Was there anything more than graffiti?' I asked, remembering what Karl had said about his tomatoes.

'Oh yes. Jamie was full of surprises. One was depositing dead fish into people's letterboxes. Mine in particular. Just what you want on a hot summer's day.'

'Are you sure it was him?'

'It was him, and what a delight it is that it's all stopped since Jamie died.'

'I understand Jamie broke into your home and stole some alcohol.'

'Sadly, yes.' He paused. 'Although I have no idea where he got the drugs. It was crystal meth. Did you know? The police grilled me about that. As if I'd have anything to do with drugs.'

'And Cynthia fell over on her boat. I understand you knew her well.'

He frowned. 'No,' he said. 'Hardly at all. She would stick her nose in occasionally. Playing good neighbour. I had—and wanted—nothing to do with her.'

'There seems to have been a lot of deaths...'

Philip's eyes settled on my face. 'You were saying?'

'Only that a lot of people have died.'

'Really?' Philip lowered his voice. 'Some might say that there's a serial killer at work. Except such people usually have a modus operandi. A particular victim. A method of killing. Maybe even take a trophy from the murder.' He shrugged. 'But all we have here is a series of random, unconnected deaths.'

He stared at me, and I met his gaze steadily. *Is he baiting me?* The sound of the nearby waves fell away as the remoteness of this location struck me. Here I was perched on this lonely section of coast. What if Philip Taylor were that killer? No one had seen us walk around here. I could be sitting alone with a maniac.

Trixie barked. She could always sense when I was uncomfortable. The sound seemed to break the spell as Philip's face twisted into a grin. 'You're thinking I could be a killer?' he said. 'That maybe I murdered all those people for kicks?'

'I think you have an overactive imagination.' I didn't like being mocked. 'As you say, all those deaths are unconnected.'

'Maybe. But I've been watching people. Playing detective.'

'And what have you discovered?'

'Nothing. If this were a detective story, the killers would be Nola and Monica. It's always the person you least suspect.'

I didn't answer.

'Or maybe it's me,' Philip continued. 'Maybe I haven't been playing detective at all. Maybe I like killing people.'

'Did you kill those people?' I asked flatly.

The air was very still as Philip studied my face.

'Of course not,' he said.

'You're not working at the moment?'

'I'm retired,' he said. 'I retired early.'

'You're very young to retire, and this is a quiet place. Why are you living here when there's a world out there?'

Philip looked away. 'I don't like crowds,' he said. 'I don't like *people*, truth be known. The fewer people I have around me, the better.'

Looks like your wish is coming true.

11

Yawning, I pulled into the driveway of Nan's home. It was late afternoon, and I was exhausted. Heading inside, I called out, but there was no answer. I glanced at my watch. She would normally be around at this time.

Trixie settled into her favourite spot in the living room for a snooze while I made a cup of tea. A car pulled into the driveway next door, and my daughter Amanda and her husband got out. I went onto the front verandah.

'Hey, mum!' Amanda called out. 'Long time no see.'

'Hey!' I responded.

Amanda was a younger, prettier version of me, whereas her husband Tom looked like a born salesman. They ran the town's most successful real estate agency: Cape Real Estate. I asked if they'd seen Nan.

'She's probably down at the protest,' Amanda said.

'Still?'

'The crowd's bigger than ever,' Tom said. 'The whole town's

up in arms about the boatshed.'

I sighed. 'No one cared about it for years. Then the moment people talk about knocking it down, everyone's unhappy.'

'I suppose we don't appreciate things until they're gone. Or we're at risk of losing them.'

Wishing them goodnight, I headed inside and finished my tea. My next stop was the fridge which proved to be an enormous disappointment. The only leftover food was a three-day-old lasagne. I closed the fridge door firmly and settled on the couch.

I felt vaguely depressed. My investigation into what had happened at Port Logan was going nowhere. I'd interviewed a bunch of people. Any of them could have committed a series of murders—or not. Maybe there wasn't a killer in the town. Perhaps the whole thing was just a series of random deaths. These things did happen. Maybe Port Logan was an unlucky town.

I checked my phone, flicking through emails and then my calendar.

Oh no, I thought. *You've got to be kidding.*

'I've really got to set this thing up to give me alerts,' I told Trixie.

She lifted her head sleepily.

'I'm having dinner with George, Sadie, and Todd in an hour,' I told her. 'Do you think I feel like going?'

Trixie's ears perked up.

'That's right,' I told her. 'No.' Unfortunately, there was no way I could get out of it. I couldn't cancel. It would upset everyone if I did. 'Will you go to dinner on my behalf?'

She shook her head.

'Yeah,' I said. 'Didn't think so.'

I headed to the bathroom, had a quick shower, and was soon changed into a petite black dress. I'd arranged to meet Todd at George and Sadie's place, but now I was rethinking that. If I turned up early, it meant I had to deal with them alone. If I were late, it meant Todd had to speak to people he barely knew. We were better off turning up together.

A minute later, I was on my phone. 'Todd? Do you mind if I come to your place and you drive?'

'Sure. No problem.'

I got Todd's address. After grabbing a bottle of wine to regift to George and Sadie, I left Trixie behind and headed out the door. A few minutes later, I pulled up in front of Todd's place. It was a ramshackle weatherboard home a street back from the beach. Not what I'd expected. Overgrown around the edges, the lawn in front was neatly trimmed. He was already out front when I arrived.

Now that I was here, my curiosity was piqued. I'd known Todd for months now and had no idea how he lived. 'You're not giving me a tour?' I asked.

Laughing, he led me in through the front door. If I were expecting a wild and crazy bachelor's pad, I was destined to be disappointed. His place was surprisingly organised. The furniture was modern, and everything was dusted. The carpet was clean. Unsurprisingly, one room was a dedicated gym. Although my experience with weight sets was minimal, his looked professional. Todd's kitchen was clean, with a few tins of protein powder neatly lined up on the bench. A couple of decent Australian landscape paintings decorated the living room.

'An old friend of mine from school painted them,' he said. 'She sells them for quite a lot these days.'

His dog, Rocko, a three-legged greyhound, came silently into the room. As I gave him a pat, I pointed to a closed door leading off the living room. 'What's in there?'

Todd rolled his eyes. 'You know curiosity killed the cat?'

'It's in my genes!'

'Promise you won't laugh?'

Todd went to the door and cracked it open.

'I promise,' I said. 'Although, I don't know why—*you've got to be kidding!*'

A trainset ran from one end of the room to the other. The tracks ran through small towns, forests, valleys, and hills. The walls along the outside had been painted either as sky or distant mountains.

The detail was fantastic. Everything looked unerringly like someone had made a miniature version of the landscape. There were three trains, and these were to the same proportion as the buildings, which were the same proportion as the hills and rivers. Standing at one of the miniature stations were people waiting to board a train. Another train was emerging from a tunnel. The third was crossing a bridge. The whole landscape appeared to be a cross between British and Australian-themed terrains. Along one side was a section of the coast, complete with sparkling acrylic water.

'How...who...why...' I couldn't seem to find words. 'Did you do this?'

'It took a while.' Todd actually seemed to be turning red. 'A few years.'

'This is amazing!' I crossed to the nearest section. 'It's so realistic.'

'You've seen train sets before?'

'I've done a few stories on local enthusiasts. This is the best I've seen.'

Todd grinned. 'Thanks.'

I turned to him. 'Why did you not tell me about this?'

'It never came up in conversation,' he said, shrugging.

'*What?*' I punched his arm.

'Ouch! What was that for?'

'That's for keeping secrets!' I said. 'Especially a secret like this! It's like entering the land of Oz. It's fantastic!' I studied him a little more closely. 'Why have you not mentioned this before?'

Todd shrugged. 'Not everyone understands this kind of hobby,' he explained. 'Some people think it's ridiculous. You know, a grown man playing with trains.'

I could understand his concern. He was a senior cop in our community. A pillar of our town. He was also a big guy. A big, loveable bear of a guy with powerfully thick arms. Even his fingers were solid. He was a giant against the miniature landscape.

This is what Todd does in his spare time, I thought.

A workbench sat to one side. On it was a tiny train, caboose, and something that looked like a half-completed building. I could visualise Todd here in the quiet hours, painting the building or checking some tiny detail. A big man putting his heart into something unique and charming.

I peered at the diorama. 'This isn't ridiculous,' I said. 'It's a work of art.'

Todd stared at me. 'Thanks,' he said softly.

For one long moment, I thought he would kiss me, and somewhere in the back of my mind, I thought that would be okay. This was a whole different side of Todd I'd never seen before. The private side. The side that other people didn't get to see.

'I feel privileged to be invited to Lilliput,' I said.

'You're the first person I've brought here.'

'None of your cop friends have seen this?' He shook his head, so I continued. 'You know that Jim Turner plays a board game involving steam-driven cars and dinosaurs?'

'I know, and I never ridicule him.'

This made me think.

Maybe I need to be more understanding too.

My phone beeped, and I glanced at it. 'Looks like we'd better get going,' I said. 'Sadie's wonderful cooking awaits.'

We went out to his car, a white Holden Commodore. Todd's phone rang, and he glanced at the screen. 'Hold on,' he said. 'I'd better take this.'

It looked like police business, so I stepped away a few feet to let him take the call. After a couple of minutes, he hung up and gave me a sheepish expression.

'Rosie,' he said. 'Bad news. I've got to go into work.'

'What?'

'I'm sorry. Some of the team is off sick at the moment, and now we've had someone else call in ill. I can't leave the station that short-staffed.'

I understood although I was bitterly disappointed. 'Okay,' I said. 'You go off and play cops and robbers, and I'll go to dinner.'

'Don't be like that.'

'Sorry.' I sighed. 'You're doing the right thing. Thanks for being a good guy.'

'Comes with the territory.'

Wishing him goodnight, I returned to my car and headed down the street.

I'd only gone half a block when I thought about what lay ahead. Walking in the door of George's place without a date wasn't just a bad look. It was downright embarrassing, almost as if I hadn't gotten on with my life.

What can I do?

I thought hard for a moment before inspiration struck. 'Hang on,' I muttered. Pulling over, I grabbed out my phone and found a number. It was answered on the third ring.

'Keith?' I said. 'It's Rosie.'

'Hey, Rosie.' His voice came back, unexpectedly warm and welcoming. 'What a surprise.'

I explained my dilemma to him, half-expecting him to say it was ridiculously short notice.

'Dinner?' Keith said. 'I never say no to food. Sure, I'll come.'

'Really?' I let out a long breath. 'Thank goodness. Can I pick you up?'

I'd caught him in the middle of a walk down Percy Street. Within minutes, I had him in the car, and we were zooming through town.

'You're a lifesaver,' I said.

'Hey, the pleasure's all mine. I was going to spend the night walking the streets of Cape Carson alone, and now I'm out with a beautiful woman.'

I accepted the compliment graciously.

'So George is a good cook?' Keith said.

'His family's Greek, so he can throw together a decent moussaka or souvlaki,' I said. 'Other than that, he's pretty hopeless. I imagine Sadie's been doing a lot of the cooking.'

'And what's Nico like?'

I sighed. 'Not one of my favourite people. Not a bad guy but a terrible plumber. He doesn't focus enough on what he's doing. George was always a better tradesman.' I thought. 'Sadie might be cooking tonight. I'm not sure. We'll have to see.'

We drove through town. Nico was one of those people I'd say hello to when I saw him around town. Other than that, I avoided him. In fact, more than once, I'd steered clear of him by crossing to the other side of the road.

Pulling up in front of the house, I expected it to look as derelict as usual but was pleasantly surprised. Nico had no idea how to make a yard look nice, and George wasn't much better. It was his previous girlfriend, Blossom, who'd tried to bring the yard in order by planting some fruit trees and other shrubs.

Since she'd moved on, the place had taken another step up. The lawn was mowed, and the trees and shrubs were more advanced. It almost looked homely. Maybe Sadie had taken over the upgrading of Nico's home. If she had, she was doing a good job.

'Wow,' I said as we got out of the jeep.

'You're surprised?'

'Back in the old days, you could have mistaken this place for the local dump.'

There was a frantic barking as we approached the door, and a voice called out.

'Calm down!' Sadie yelled. 'We all know you can make noise!' The door flew open, and Sadie stood there, beaming at us. 'You made it!'

'We're here,' I said unnecessarily. 'I didn't bring Trixie.'

'That's a shame. Maybe next time.'

I introduced Keith, and Sadie had the good sense not to mention that I'd suddenly had a change of date. 'Any friend of Rosie's is a friend of ours,' she said.

We followed Sadie inside, and this was where it got really surprising. The interior was clean. *Amazing.* One time I'd been here, there had literally been nowhere to sit. I had to remain standing the whole time. Now it was like a functional house, light and airy with polished floors and not a piece of rubbish in sight.

We headed through the living room and out the back, where Nico and George were at the barbeque. Nico raised a can of beer. 'Hey!' he said. 'Now we can get this party started!'

Good grief, I thought.

Nico looked like a wreck. He had about a week's growth and hadn't ironed the Hawaiian shirt he was wearing. His shorts were stained from where a pen had leaked.

I introduced Keith to him and George. Glancing around the backyard, I was surprised to see it free of junk. The last time I'd been here, it had been piled high with stacks of timber and pipes.

This is amazing.

Sadie brought out some drinks.

'I've got to say,' I confided to her, 'this place is looking pretty good.'

'Habitable?'

'More than. How did you train these guys to keep things clean?'

'It took a lot,' Sadie said with mock seriousness. 'Cattle prods. Beatings. It took some doing, but now I just need to ring a bell, and they start vacuuming.'

I burst out laughing. Sadie was genuinely funny. Maybe, just as importantly, she was a no-nonsense person. I could see why this relationship was working for George. He could be a bit directionless sometimes. Having a decent woman to keep him on the straight and narrow would be good for him.

George turned over some sausages on the barbeque. 'Glad

you could make it,' he said. 'Now you can see how my cooking's improved.'

'It's not hard to cook a sausage,' I advised him. 'Although you did turn an entire barbeque to charcoal one time.'

My ex-husband said hello to Keith, and they shook hands. 'That charcoal barbeque wasn't my fault,' George said. 'Well, not *entirely* my fault. I had lighter fluid sitting beside the barbeque, and it fell over and exploded. Not one of my finer moments.'

'But it was nice seeing all those firemen,' I said innocently. 'And the house only got slightly singed.'

I turned my attention to Nico, who let out a raucous laugh. 'Rosie!' he said. 'Beautiful lady!'

Nico hugged me and tried to lift me off the ground. There were a few problems with this scenario. The first was that I didn't want to be picked up. The second was that Nico was six inches shorter than me. The third was that he wasn't able to lift me. The fourth issue, and possibly the worst of all, was that he stunk of beer and smelt like he hadn't washed since the turn of the century. The party had obviously started for him several hours before anyone else.

Nico turned his attention to Keith. 'And you're the new bloke on the block!' he said. 'Good on ya, mate!'

Keith's face was expressionless. 'Nice to meet you.'

They shook hands, and Nico went to grab another beer. I

glanced over at Keith to see what he made of all this. He simply raised an eyebrow.

This could be a long night, I thought.

12

'So you had a good time?' Kim said, incredulously.

'I know it sounds hard to believe,' I said. 'But we ended up having a ball.'

It was the following day, and we were sitting at a table outside Sandy's Diner. Trixie was at my feet, lapping water from a metal bowl. The bay was flat and still, and I was on a high from the previous night. I'd texted Kim early to see if she could join me for the day, and she'd agreed as the library renovations were still ongoing.

'We played charades,' I explained.

'That can be good fun,' Kim said. 'I used to play that with my kids. What did you have to act out?'

'Well...' I started giggling.

'What?'

'I had to act out the word *trampoline*, but Keith...' I couldn't stop laughing. 'He had...he had...'

'What?'

'He had *party pooper!*'

Kim almost fell off her chair laughing. Once we'd both sobered up, she took a sip of her cappuccino and leaned close.

'Rosie,' Kim said. 'We need to talk.'

'We are talking.'

'I mean about Todd and Keith. What's going on? How many guys are you dating?'

'There's a few dozen,' I said. 'No. Seriously. You know how it is. It's either feast or famine.'

'And have you told Todd about going to the barbeque with Keith?'

'Er, not quite.'

'Will you tell him?'

'I...I'm not sure. I'll see.' This was too uncomfortable for me to talk about right now. My love life was so complicated, even I had no idea what was going on, so I changed subjects. 'You know the council meeting's coming up about the boatshed?'

'I know. The Historical Society has asked me to speak at the meeting.'

Kim was the library's local history expert.

'What are you going to say?' I asked.

Kim sighed. 'I've written a speech,' she said. 'But you know I hate public speaking.'

'You always do an excellent job,' I said. 'You'll be great.'

'Thanks for your vote of confidence. So what's our next

step?'

I'd already been thinking about this. 'The only people I haven't spoken to are Jamie's parents: Robert and Jean Farrell,' I said. 'Maybe they can shed some light on his death.'

We finished our coffees, went to my jeep, and were soon heading over to Port Logan. Trixie stuck her head out the window, and her ears flapped wildly in the wind. I'd never been this way so many times in one week, and I doubted I'd ever do so again. No matter how things turned out, Port Logan was too strange for my liking.

We parked outside of Robert and Jean's place. I hadn't looked closely at it before, so I'd thought it was a falling down shack like many of the others. Now I realised it was different: the building was in a state of renovation. The roof was new. So were the windows. The decking on the veranda had also been replaced. We knocked at the front door, and it was answered almost immediately by a man with unruly long hair and a pointed chin.

'Robert Farrell?' I said.

His face fell. 'Oh,' he said. 'You must be the journalists.'

'I'm the photographer,' Kim explained.

'Whatever. We're not interested in talking to you.'

He started to close the door.

'Please,' I said. 'I just want to understand what happened to your son.'

'I know what happened to him,' Robert Farrell said. 'He took drugs and died.'

'Are you sure?'

His eyes narrowed, but before he could answer, a woman's voice came from inside the house. 'What are you saying?' She moved into view. Shorter than her husband, Jean had eyes that were soft and brown and prematurely greying hair styled in a pixie cut.

'I've been looking into the history of the town.' I didn't want to spill the beans, but there didn't seem to be any way around this. I needed these people to speak to me. 'It seems a lot of people have died in Port Logan. More than seems reasonable.'

'So you're saying...' Jean began. 'What *are* you saying?'

'I wonder if there's another explanation for Jamie's death.' I quickly added, 'I don't know what that could be. I'm hoping you can help clear up some things.'

Robert began. 'We don't need you raking up—'

'Come in,' Jean said, giving her husband a sideways glance. 'We need to hear what they have to say.'

Minutes later, we were ensconced in their living room. The inside was similar to what was going on outside. Some of the rooms had been renovated, but the living room was still original; there was an enormous hole in the floor. Trixie sniffed around the hole and I pulled her away from it.

'Your place is lovely,' Kim said.

'Thanks,' Robert said flatly and turned to his wife. 'I'm going out. You can speak to them if you want.'

Jean didn't bother trying to convince him otherwise. She turned to us apologetically as soon as the front door had shut behind him.

'I'm sorry about Robert,' she said. 'Jamie's death has been hard.'

'We're sorry about what happened,' I said.

'I suppose everyone's told you about Jamie,' Jean said. 'That he was an out-of-control teenager who terrorised the whole town. That's not true. He had his problems. We suspect it was undiagnosed ADHD.'

'I see.'

'The older Jamie got, the more out of control he became. Half the town was up in arms about him. Some people were so sick and tired of him that they yelled abuse when they saw us on the street.'

'I understand he had a run-in with Ray Pennington.'

'Not just him,' Jean sighed, pushing back her greying hair. 'Jamie did something to Karl Hoffman's garden. Broke the front window of Iris's shop. Spraypainted Grace and Cynthia's front walls. Smashed ornaments in Nola and Monica's yard. Put a dead animal into Philip's letterbox. Killed one of Sybil and Stewart's trees.'

Good grief, I thought. *It's a wonder Jamie lived as long as he did!*

'We were trying to get help for Jamie,' Jean continued. 'But I work at a nursing home, and Robert's a bricklayer. We've been away a lot. The doctors said nothing was wrong with Jamie, so we'd discipline him. Not let him watch TV. Take away his phone.'

'Did he have friends?' Kim asked.

'Yes, but he was always fighting with them. We spoke to the school counsellors. Even they didn't know what to do.' She paused. 'Part of the problem was the lack of kids Jamie's age around here. It's an older crowd. It meant Jamie had nothing to do. He'd come home on the bus and be alone for hours. We wouldn't get back till late.'

Sounds like a recipe for disaster, I thought.

'Do you mind if I ask you about Jamie's death?' I said.

Jean's lips pursed. 'It was towards the end of summer,' she said. 'Robert and I had been at work for the day. Robert got home ahead of me. He usually did.

'That afternoon, he'd started making dinner. I asked where Jamie was, but he hadn't seen hide nor hair of him. That wasn't unusual. Jamie was often out somewhere.

'I tried calling him on his phone, but Jamie didn't answer. That was unusual. Like most teenagers, he never went any-where without his phone, so I went out searching. I checked the path leading up to Piper Beach. You probably know that's where poor Stewart was killed recently. It was along there that I bumped into Philip. That's when the trouble started.'

'What do you mean?' Kim asked.

'Philip said there'd been a break-in at his house and a bottle of scotch had been stolen. He said he'd seen Jamie nearby. I said it couldn't be him, though to be honest, I wasn't sure. You see, Jamie had broken into Grace's home a few weeks before. She'd actually caught him in the act and had been good about it. Instead of calling the police, Grace gave him some biscuits and a glass of milk.'

'She seems like a nice woman,' I said.

'Grace is one of the nicest people around here.' Jean seemed lost in her own thoughts for a moment. 'Anyway, Philip and I got into an argument. I don't remember what we said. He eventually walked off in a huff and I continued looking for Jamie.

'I was starting to get worried by now, so I took the path around to the other side of the bay to Cullen Beach. There was no sign of him. I wasn't sure what to do then, and he still wasn't answering his phone. That's when I decided to search the dunes. There's a track that leads up from the beach. It comes around in a wide loop and back to town.'

The woman's eyes grew distant. 'I bumped into Grace on the track,' she continued. 'She usually goes around that track in a clockwise direction, but this time she'd only made it halfway around because it was getting dark. She hadn't seen Jamie. I thought he could have been out in the dunes getting drunk. That's what he'd done one other time.

'It was getting late by now, so I rang Robert to see if Jamie had turned up, and he hadn't. I kept following the track around through the dunes. It's lonely out there. Scary, sometimes, too.'

'We've heard stories about the monster,' Kim ventured.

'I don't believe in the monster,' Jean said. 'Although plenty of people do.'

'Did you see anyone else in the dunes?' I asked.

'No, although I've seen Ray Pennington painting out there sometimes. I suppose I was thinking of Ray when I was searching. If he'd encountered Jamie alone, something could have happened.'

'What do you mean?'

Jean shrugged. 'Anything,' she said. 'I just felt afraid. Ray's a grown man, and Jamie was a difficult teenager. I continued to the point where the bush starts to thicken. A post sticks out of the ground there.' She stopped, her eyes haunted. 'That's when I saw him. Just a flash of his sleeve in the dunes. I called his name, but he didn't answer. I thought he'd fallen asleep, or was drunk and couldn't hear me, so I plodded across the dune to where he was lying. And there he was.'

And there he was.

The words echoed in my mind. It was a terrible thought, and I couldn't imagine the horror of Jean finding her son out there.

I finally spoke. 'The police said that he'd drunk the Scotch and taken crystal meth?'

'The scotch came from Philip's home,' Jean confirmed. 'Even Philip admitted that. We don't know where he got the meth. This is a drug free area.'

'Could he have gotten it from school?' Kim asked.

'His school friends were interviewed by the police. They all denied giving him the drugs.'

'Could he have stolen them from Philip's home?' I asked.

'That's what I thought too,' Jean said. 'Except Philip denied it, though I suppose he would. Just because you're a university educated professor doesn't mean you don't take drugs.' She stopped. 'But I've got to say this: Philip came to see us after Jamie died and told us the meth wasn't his. I don't know why, but I believed him.'

I thought hard. 'You saw Grace out that way,' I said. 'Could she have given it to him?'

Jean shrugged. 'Why would she? And where would she get it? Grace said she saw Jamie but not anyone else. Though if you're on that track, and you see someone coming, you can just duck off to one side, and no one would see you.'

So, where did Jamie get the drugs?

'There's one other thing that's never made any sense,' she said. 'It's Jamie's phone. It wasn't with him when he was found, and it's never turned up.'

That was strange. I thanked Jean for her time, promising that the article I put together would be respectful of her and her family. Kim, Trixie, and I headed out onto the street and stood in the sun. It seemed exceptionally sunny after being inside the quiet house. There was no sign of Robert. Or anyone else, for that matter. The town seemed abandoned as if everyone had left.

'What now?' Kim asked.

'I'd like to take a look at the sand dunes,' I said.

We decided to take the same path that Jean had followed. We trailed around the west side of the bay and took the path up and over the hill. The fencing behind the houses was similar to the other side of the bay: either non-existent or unsteady constructions of timber and wire. Although both Grace and the Pennington homes were new, not a lot of care had been taken with the rear fences. The gaping holes were big enough to allow anyone to walk through.

And that wouldn't be a problem. Not out here. This was a quiet corner of the world. Hardly anyone visited the town, let alone wandered around these lonely dunes. We followed the trail through the hills of sand until the ground grew harder. On one side were rolling, sandy hills leading down to the sea. The other side was sandy too, but with spinifex and huge banks of coast wattle.

It's eerie out here.

'Wow,' Kim said. 'Jean was right about hiding places. The killer—if there were a killer—could have ducked away behind a bush, and no one would have seen them. It reminds me of that movie, The Sand Dune Killer.'

I gave her a look. 'Do you have to mention that now?'

Kim sighed. 'Just saying.'

We continued along the trail. Just as it inclined over a hill, I spotted a post sticking out of the ground in a nearby sand dune.

'That must be where Jean found her son,' I said.

Leaving the trail, we trooped across the sand until we reached the post. From here, the houses of Port Logan were out of sight. Beyond the mounds of sand, you could glimpse the beach and the water stretching away in both directions. There was no trail here, though. It wasn't even a stopping-off point. The post appeared to be the final remnant of an old timber fence. There was nothing to distinguish this part of the endless sea of dunes except...

'This is weird,' I said. 'I've got the strangest feeling of déjà vu, like I've been here before.'

'My cousin Alice used to get that all the time.'

'Really?'

'Yes. It turned out to be a brain tumour. One time, Alice thought she was Winston Churchill.'

I sighed. 'Great,' I said. 'That makes me feel better.'

Ready to head back to town, I was casting my gaze around the dunes one last time when I glanced down at the base of the post. I scraped away some sand.

'What is it?' Kim asked.

'A piece of knotted rope.' I examined it more closely. 'It's quite intricate.'

Kim brought up a list of knots on her phone. 'Okay,' she said slowly. 'For a start, that's not one piece of rope. It's two. The knot's called a carrick bend. It's used to connect two pieces of rope.'

'Does it say when it's used?'

'Anywhere, by the look of it, but most often on ships. It's also known as the Sailor's breastplate.'

What's it doing here?

'Ray Pennington's had experience with ships,' I said.

'So did Cynthia Shepherd.'

'I suppose anyone could have left this here.'

'Even Jamie.'

It could be the killer's calling card or it could have nothing at all to do with the case. It could have been tied to the post at any time by anyone. Trixie sniffed my hand. I absently slipped her a doggy snack as I glanced about. The same feeling of déjà vu was tugging at my senses. I'd never been here before, and yet I knew this place.

How can I recognise a place I've never seen?

13

Kar-rooom!

Opening my eyes, I stared into the darkness as my heart thudded wildly.

Where am I?

Slowly, it all came back. I was in the basement flat of Nola and Monica's home in Port Logan. It was night, and Kim was still asleep.

Lightning cast an iridescent rectangle of light across the floor, followed seconds later by a groaning rumble of thunder. I crossed to the window and gazed out. A storm was raging outside, and rain was coming down in bucketloads. A single light, hanging from a street pole at the jetty, was swinging back and forth in the wind.

My goodness, I thought. *What a night!*

Rain had been threatening for days, and now it had finally arrived. Sitting on the window seat, I glanced over at Kim. She was dead to the world, which was a shame because she loved storms. Although her idea of the perfect storm would be one where something ghostly or monstrous was prowling about in the dark.

I glanced at my phone: *1.13am*.

Most of the town was in darkness, but a few lights were on at various houses. A light was on at the Pennington's house. Also at Karl and Sybil's places. They may have been woken by the storm as well. I rested my head against the timber window frame. It was cool against my face.

I'd just give it another moment and…

I blinked.

Goodness.

I'd fallen asleep again. I checked my phone: *2.34am*. Looking out the window, I saw the storm had stopped, the ground was wet, and the town lay in darkness. All the lights were out now except for the one at the jetty. I was about to return to bed when I looked more closely. The light *was* still on at Sybil's place, and something was moving down there.

The monster?

Don't be ridiculous. The monster isn't real!

A bulky figure was in her doorway. A man? Probably. I couldn't be sure. I hissed Kim's name, but her only response was steady breathing.

'Thanks for nothing,' I muttered.

Trixie raised her head, but I gave her a pat and told her to go back to sleep. I threw on some clothing and was out the door in seconds. Although the air was still after the storm, waves crashed and surged into the tiny bay. The streetlight reflected tiny moons in the puddles around the jetty as I approached Sybil's place.

There was movement in Sybil's open doorway. She was talking to someone, a man by the look of it.

'Don't threaten me!' she said. 'I'm not doing this anymore!'

The man murmured in a low voice.

Sybil spoke again. 'I don't care about your money! Now—get out!'

The light in the hallway dimmed, and I realised the man was leaving. I dived into the nearby bushes and hid as the figure came barrelling down the path. Holding my breath, I finally raised my head to see that the door to Sybil's home had closed. The man who she'd argued with was stalking up the hill.

I waited until he was almost out of sight before racing back to the street. When I was halfway up the hill, there was the roar of an engine. I ran the rest of the way, but I was too late. A sedan was already disappearing out of sight.

What was all that about? I wondered. *A lover's tiff? Or something worse?*

Stewart Bard hadn't been dead long. Was Sybil already in another relationship? Was she arguing with her new boyfriend? That didn't explain her comment about money.

Did she owe someone money? Or did they owe her?

Standing in the dark wouldn't give me any answers, so I headed back to Nola and Monica's place. I closed the door quietly, crept across to the bed, and was almost there when my foot caught on a stray item of clothing.

What the—?

I tripped and crashed to the floor. Lying there quietly, my eyes open like a fox in the night, I waited for Kim to berate me.

She let out a long snore.

Kim, I thought. *You'd sleep through an atomic explosion!*

Climbing into bed, I was asleep in minutes. The next morning, I awoke to find Kim emerging from the bathroom.

'Hey you,' she said. 'Are you ever getting out of bed? I've been up for ages. I'll make coffee.'

'Coffee would be good,' I groaned.

Although it was instant coffee, anything would do first thing in the morning. I told Kim about my nightly escapade.

She handed me a cup. 'You should have woken me.'

'You sleep like the dead!'

'No, I don't.'

'Kim. You were so sound asleep I thought you were in a coma. I almost rang an ambulance.'

'Whatever. Anyway, what do you make of this guy who was threatening Sybil?'

I told her I had no idea. 'It was something to do with money,'

I said. 'And Sybil wasn't happy.'

Kim glanced at her watch. 'Let's get a move-on,' she said. 'Trixie's been up for ages. I'm sure she's dying for a walk.'

Gulping down my coffee, I showered, got dressed, and we were soon standing out the front. Trixie gave a happy pant. Her doggy sense of smell was enjoying the crisp early morning sea air. Iris's shop had just opened for the day. She was putting out her A-frame sign. The woman gave us a nod, and we waved.

'Another day at the museum,' Kim muttered.

'Makes you wonder how she stays in business.'

The front door of Nola and Monica's place cracked open, and the old ladies peered out.

'Good morning, girls,' Monica said.

We chorused *good morning*.

'We survived another night,' Nola informed us. 'When you get to our age, waking up's always a surprise.'

'We haven't woken up dead,' Monica added. 'Not yet, anyway.'

The two ladies laughed. Wishing them a good day, Kim and I made our way to the jetty. On the other side of the bay, Ray and Robyn had just left their home. Ray gave us a wave as they turned and took the west path towards the beach. On our side, Philip emerged from his house and turned for East Head.

'Another exciting day in Port Logan,' I murmured.

'However will we cope?' Kim replied.

Trixie gave me a long stare. She always did that when she was impatient. 'Are you bored too?' I asked her. 'Maybe we can go to the beach.'

She made the same sound again. This time, I noticed the sound of distant howling. *Where's that coming from?* Trixie gave a short bark.

'What is it, girl?' I asked.

'Something's up,' Kim said.

Trixie tugged at her lead, and we followed her along the path to Karl Hoffman's home. This was the source of the howling. Kim and I silently exchanged glances. There was something disconcerting about that sound.

'Come on,' I said.

We mounted the steps to find the front door slightly ajar. 'Karl?' I called.

No answer came from within, so we continued into the hallway. It was immediately apparent that the source of the sound was Karl's dog, Sirius. She was locked in one of the rooms. Kim grabbed my arm as I reached for the handle.

'Rosie,' she said. 'Look!'

The kitchen was at the end of the hall. A pair of feet were visible. We cautiously crept down to find Karl's body splayed on the floor. A chair was upturned, and the back door was open. A revolver lay near his left hand. He'd been shot in the head at close range.

'Is he...' Kim began.

'Dead,' I confirmed. 'Supposedly by suicide.'

'Supposedly?'

'This story just got a whole lot bigger,' I said. 'Look at the table.'

On the table lay a piece of knotted rope. It looked to be the same texture and thickness as the one we'd found out in the dunes.

'That can't be a coincidence,' Kim said.

'I agree.' I snapped a photo of it with my phone. 'It's the killer's calling card.'

After ringing Todd, it only took a few minutes for two police cars to arrive. By then, Kim and I were waiting outside.

Todd strode up to us. 'Another one?' he said. 'Is that all you do with your time, Rosie? Search for dead people?'

'Kim was with me this time,' I said defensively.

Todd shot her a look.

'Hey!' Kim said. 'Where she goes, I go.'

Without saying another word, the policeman went inside to investigate the crime scene. Constable Turner arrived and got a statement from us. By then, the other locals of Port Logan had gathered behind a line of police tape. We crossed to them.

'What's happened?' Monica asked. 'What's happened to Karl?'

I cast my gaze over the sea of faces: Nola was there too, of course. So were the Farrells.

Iris had closed up her shop, although this probably would have been her biggest trading day ever, with a record number of people in town. Ray Pennington and Robyn huddled together at the back of the group, along with Grace, Philip, and Sybil.

I told them that Karl was dead, which started an immediate commotion.

'Was it an accident?' Ray asked.

'Or was he murdered?' Nola asked, obviously relishing the idea. 'Imagine. A murder right here in Port Logan.'

'Yes,' Kim said, catching my eye. 'Imagine that.'

Grace stared. 'What happened to him?'

'It was an accident,' Sybil said. 'Wasn't it, Rosie?'

All eyes turned to me. 'It's too early to say,' I told them. 'The police will determine a cause of death.'

I tried to read their faces. No one looked guilty, although I supposed a real killer would be able to hide that. Grabbing Kim's arm, I drew her back to where Constable Turner was standing. 'Jim,' I said. 'When Todd has a free moment, can you tell him I have some information about Karl's death?'

He frowned. 'This isn't a confession, is it, Rosie?'

'Sure it is, and I'm flying to the moon next week.'

'So—not a confession.'

The constable disappeared inside. Checking the image of

the knot on her phone, Kim finally gave a tiny nod. 'It's a bowline,' she murmured. 'Used all the time on ships.'

Todd emerged after a few minutes, wearing blue latex gloves. 'What is it, Rosie? Jim said you've got some information.'

Kim and I glanced over to the waiting crowd and turned our backs for privacy. We told him about the piece of knotted rope on the table and how we had found a similar piece up in the sand dunes.

'All right,' Todd said uncertainly. 'I'll take a look. It could just be a coincidence, though. We are on the coast.'

There was no point arguing or trying to convince Todd. Everything would become clear soon enough. 'That's fine. Kim and I are going for a walk. Ring if you need anything.'

Kim, Trixie, and I traipsed up the hill to where Oxley Street turned onto Millicent Drive. A coroner's vehicle trundled past us.

'What are we doing?' Kim asked.

'Checking our theory.' We reached the crest of the hill where Florence Teale had been run over. 'We're looking for a piece of knotted rope,' I said. 'Something similar to what we found at the other crime scenes.'

'Rosie,' Kim said, nudging me. 'You mean something like that?'

I followed her gaze. The street sign pointing down the hill was like any other. No one would have looked twice at it.

What made this different was the length of knotted rope at the bottom. A piece of rope, weathered by the elements, unnoticed by anyone.

'It's a rolling hitch,' Kim confirmed as she took a photo. 'Another sailing knot.'

'It's definitely the killer's calling card.'

'What now?'

'Now I ring Todd,' I said. 'We've got a serial killer on the loose.'

14

After telling Todd what we'd found, we headed back into town to continue our investigation. The first people we spoke to were Ray and Robyn Pennington.

'That's terrible news about Karl,' Ray said, standing in his doorway. Police were still filing in and out of Karl's home. Police tape surrounded the whole property, and the entire section of path was closed off. They were doing a full forensic examination of the scene. 'I don't know who would have killed him.'

'How do you know it's murder?' I asked.

Robyn was standing at his side. She nodded to the hive of activity. 'They wouldn't do that for a suicide,' she said. 'Or an accidental death. Karl was murdered. No doubt about it.'

'Do you mind if I ask where you were last night?'

'Home,' Ray said. 'Why do you ask?'

'Just curious.'

'You weren't home the whole evening,' Kim said.

Ray frowned. 'What makes you say that?'

She pointed to the ground under their car. 'It rained last night,' Kim said. 'The ground under your car should be dry, but it's wet. Someone took your car out and returned it later.'

I glanced sideways at Kim.

You're a genius, girl!

This was met with a long silence as neither person answered or even looked at each other.

'It was me,' Robyn finally confessed. 'I went for a drive.'

'Really?' Ray said. 'Where?'

'Nowhere. I just needed to clear my head.'

People did that sort of thing, I knew. Drove around aimlessly to sort out ideas. However, it seemed a surprise to Ray that his wife had gone out. Possibly he didn't know her as well as he thought.

'About what time was that?' I asked.

Robyn thought. 'Maybe about three.'

That's pretty late to be driving about to clear your head.

'So you didn't see Karl?'

'At three in the morning? He would have been dead to the world.' She stopped, realising what she'd just said. 'No. There was no one about.'

I didn't believe her, and Ray didn't seem convinced either, judging by his frown. Thanking the couple, Kim, Trixie, and I continued back down the coastal path.

'Well,' I said. 'A drive at three in the morning.'

'Why would she be out at that time?'

'I can only think of one reason.' I thought for a moment. 'No. Two reasons. One would be to kill Karl Hoffman. The other would be to meet someone.'

'At three in the morning? That's risky. What if her husband woke up?'

'He could be a heavy sleeper.' I fixed my gaze at her. 'Like someone I know.'

Kim ignored me. 'So Robyn could be meeting a lover.'

'Maybe.'

Trying to work out who that could be was like searching for a needle in a haystack. With internet dating and apps on phones where you swiped left, right, and up and down, her special friend could be anyone.

We continued to Iris's shop. It was open now, or what passed for open. A constable was just heading out with a bottle of soft drink as we arrived. Iris was back at her position behind the counter, staring out the window.

'First time anything like that's happened here,' Iris said as we entered. 'This is a peaceful town.'

Knowing the trouble that was about to come crashing down on Port Logan, all I could do was agree and nod. Once the news got out, the media frenzy that erupted would be unlike anything we'd seen before in our tiny corner of the world.

'Did you notice anything unusual last night?' I asked.

'Only the storm, although...'

I waited.

'I saw someone going into Karl's place,' she said.

'What time?' Kim asked.

'Around midnight. Maybe a little after.'

'You didn't recognise them?' I asked.

The woman pursed her lips. 'Well,' she said. 'I did, and I didn't. It was dark, and the person wore one of those big raincoats. What do you call them? Anoraks? It was dark green, almost black, with a hood. I didn't think much of it at the time, though I should have.'

'You couldn't have known anything was wrong.'

The shop owner fell silent. There was something in her expression that gave me pause.

What is she hiding?

Even Trixie tilted her head.

'Iris?' I said.

She reddened. 'I've seen that person once before. It was years ago. Although I should have come forward, I didn't.' The more she spoke, the more flushed she became. 'I've always regretted it.'

'Iris?' Kim said. 'What are you saying?'

'I saw the person in the raincoat a few years back. It was when Grace's friend was killed.'

Kim and I exchanged glances. 'When Florence Teale was run over?' I asked.

Iris nodded nervously. 'I saw the car that night,' she said. 'The one that ran her over. I didn't know that anyone had been run over. If I did, I would have rung an ambulance.'

'Iris, tell us exactly what you saw that night.'

The woman got up, crossed to the door, and turned the *Open* sign to *Closed*. 'You must promise you won't tell the police,' she said.

'We promise,' I said, although I wasn't sure we could keep that promise. 'Tell us what you saw.'

'All right. It was late, and I'd been having problems sleeping because of my allergies. Sometimes I suffer from hay fever. I got up that night to go for a walk. It settles down my hay fever, and I can get to sleep.

'I was walking up towards the dunes on the west side. It was still early evening. I'd just reached the top when I heard a bang and looked back to the other side where you turn off Millicent. I didn't see the women get hit. All I heard was a bang. You have to believe me.'

We nodded.

'What happened then?' I asked.

'The car came down the hill and up the other side. I couldn't see who was driving, but they were going at quite a pace. They tore past me and continued on into the dunes. I decided to follow at a safe distance. If I could see who was driving like a crazy person, I thought I could identify them to the police later.

'The vehicle was some distance ahead, so I lost sight of it. When I caught up, I had just reached a turn in the road when I saw a big flare of light. It was the car bursting into flames. I glimpsed a person disappearing into the dunes.'

'You didn't see what they looked like?'

'I only saw them for a second. Even then, all I saw was that same dark green coat and hood. It could have been anyone.' She stopped. 'But I'm sure it was the same person I saw going into Karl's place.'

'You've got to tell the police,' I said.

'I can't do that.'

'Why?'

'I...it's just...I don't want to get into any trouble,' Iris said. 'Any more trouble.'

Realisation struck me. 'Are you already in trouble with the police?' I asked. 'Iris, what have you done?'

The woman swallowed. 'It was years ago. I assaulted a woman who'd been my friend. She stole my boyfriend, and I attacked her. It was the wrong thing to do—I know that—but I ended up spending three years in jail.'

It must have been a serious assault, I thought.

'When did this happen?' Kim asked.

'About twenty years back.'

'Iris,' I said. 'That's a long time ago and has no bearing on this case. You must give the police this information.' I paused. 'I'm friends with the sergeant. He's new and I know he'll treat you fairly.'

'But what if he doesn't?'

'If he doesn't, then he'll be in big trouble,' I said. 'With me!'

The woman reluctantly agreed.

A few minutes later, I had returned to Karl's home, where Todd was speaking to a constable. I told him what I'd discovered.

'You're on a roll, Rosie,' he said. 'First, you find the body. Then you tell us there's a serial killer on the loose. And now you've found someone who can identify them.'

'Not identify,' I said. 'Not exactly. But you need to hear what Iris has got to say.'

15

'I'm not sure I can help you,' Philip said.

Kim and I were standing in his doorway. The man was less sure of himself than the first time I'd met him. It was as if the wind had been taken out of his sails.

'We'd like to know what you saw last night,' I said.

'I didn't see anything.'

I took a gamble. 'Someone told us they saw you out and about.'

Philip looked sick. 'Who?'

'Let us in, and we'll talk.'

At first, the man looked like he wanted to argue, but then he glanced left and right to see if anyone was watching and reluctantly allowed us in. The interior of his home was more orderly than I'd expected. Old statues sat on pedestals in the corners. Ancient parchments in frames lined the walls. Display cabinets were filled with masks from the Pacific islands.

We continued to the living room. This contained bookcases.

Lots of them. Philip obviously liked to read. The shelves were packed with books on history and archaeology.

He motioned us into lounge chairs. Trixie settled onto the floor beside me. The backdoor of his home looked out onto a garden. A vase of red and yellow gerberas sat on the windowsill of his kitchen.

I began. 'Tell us about last night.'

'You can't order me to—'

'Philip,' I cut in. 'There's an easy way, and there's a hard way. I'm good friends with the police who are investigating Karl's murder. I can have him here in sixty seconds—or you can speak to us.'

Something seemed to go out of the man as he collapsed back in his lounge chair. 'I went out last night,' he admitted. 'But there was nothing strange about it. The first time, I bought groceries, so I drove into Cape Carson. When I came home, I went to bed early.'

'What happened then?'

'I woke up in the middle of the night. I don't know what time. There was movement on the path outside. You get to recognise the sounds out there. I saw Karl passing. He gets very drunk sometimes. He was going in the direction of Piper Beach with a bottle of beer. I decided to follow.'

'Why?' Kim asked.

The man shrugged. 'I don't know,' he said. 'Something to

do. And Karl always keeps...kept...to himself. I wanted to see what he was doing.' He paused. 'Karl stopped at the edge of the water and stood there, looking out at the ocean. To be honest, I thought he was going to walk in. He was there for a while, drinking as he watched the waves. Then things got strange.

'You see,' Philip continued, 'someone else was watching Karl. I didn't see them at first. They were back there in the dunes, lying low in the sand. I only spotted them because they lifted their head.'

'Did you recognise them?' I asked.

'No. They were wearing a hood.'

A hood. I exchanged glances with Kim. That could be the same person Iris saw going into Karl's place.

'What time was this?' I asked.

'I don't know. Late. After midnight.'

'And did they see you?'

Philip nodded. 'I think so,' he said. 'Their head suddenly ducked down and they disappeared from sight. I didn't see them again.'

Thanking Philip for his time, we got up to leave. My eyes rested on the flowers in Philip's window. 'Those are lovely,' I said. 'Where did you get them?'

Philip looked surprised. 'The supermarket in Cape Carson.'

'I must get some for home.'

We started for the door.

'Rosie, I must know who saw me last night,' Philip said. 'It's important.'

'I can't tell you,' I replied. 'But I suggest you tell the police what you saw.'

We headed to the path outside. My head was aching and the day was only half done. Police were still milling around Karl's home, but not as many as before. I slipped Trixie a doggy snack as we peered out at the tiny bay.

'What do you make of all that?' I asked.

'I'd say that was a very effective bluff,' Kim said. 'Besides that, it sounds like Karl was being stalked by his killer.'

'Maybe the killer's original plan was to murder him on the beach.'

Strolling thoughtfully around the water's edge, we stopped in front of Ray and Robyn's house. I looked across at Karl's place. 'It's strange,' I said. 'I've got the same feeling of déjà vu. Like I've experienced this before.'

'A lot of these places look the same,' Kim said. 'What I'm wondering is why the killer was so intent on killing Karl.'

'Why did he—or she—kill anyone?'

'Karl could have been just another victim. Or maybe Karl knew something. Maybe he knew the killer's identity.'

'If that were true, then why invite the killer into his home? Karl was murdered in his kitchen. He knew the killer well enough to invite him in.'

'So the killer is probably local.' Kim peered around the odd assembly of houses. 'It's hard to believe that someone so insane is living here undetected.'

That was a good point. The one person who had appeared strangest had been murdered. 'I suppose we need to consider some other motive for the murders,' I said.

'Like what?'

'Well, financial gain is the most usual motive. Georgie said Ray Pennington wants to own the whole town. He got into a bidding war with Cynthia over one of the properties.'

'And Cynthia Shepherd conveniently fell on her own knife. But from what you've said, her children have no intention of selling the house. Murdering someone on the off-chance that you can buy their home seems risky. The council planning permits make new developments virtually impossible. And there doesn't seem to be any profit in killing Florence Teale or Stewart or Jamie.' She paused. 'So what other motives are there?'

I thought for a moment. 'Jealousy could be a motive,' I pointed out. 'Robyn went to see someone in the middle of the night. If that were Karl, then Ray might want him dead.'

'Yes. But that doesn't explain all the other deaths.'

'All right. What about revenge?'

Kim thought. 'That would explain most of the deaths,' she said. 'Although, of course, I mean it's an *imagined* revenge.

It could be the killer feels slighted, and it's something in their own mind for which they want revenge. Still, there's a problem with this.'

'Florence Teale?'

'Yep. Florence had been in town for all of five minutes, and the only person she knew was Grace.'

'Could someone else in town have known Florence? They knew she was coming and decided to kill her?'

'I don't see how.'

'Okay. Could Grace be the killer? Grace is the only person who knew all the victims,' I said. 'She knew Florence as well as all the local townspeople. Grace was also first on the scene when Stewart was killed, and she was in the dunes the evening Jamie died.'

'Okay,' Kim said. 'So what imagined slights could Grace have felt against all these people?'

This stumped me. 'None that I can see,' I said. 'If Grace didn't like Florence, she could have just told her not to visit. And everyone seems to get along with Grace.'

'Including Jamie.'

'That's right. Georgie said Jamie broke into Grace's home. Instead of calling the police, Grace gave him cookies and milk.'

'That hardly sounds like the actions of a cold-blooded killer.'

I agreed. Despite the warmth of the sun, I felt chilled.

A calculating mind had killed all those people, with the most likely motive being self-gratification. They *enjoyed* killing others. Maybe it was the sense of power or control that drove them. If so, it was unlikely they would ever stop.

Trixie whined, and I patted her head.

'Don't worry, girl,' I said. 'No one's getting us.'

Kim nudged me and pointed. Sybil was making her way around the bay toward her home.

'Come on,' I said. 'We need to speak to her.'

We reached Sybil just as she opened her front door. She glanced back at us. 'Oh, hello,' she said. 'I heard you two were staying in town.'

'We'd like to talk to you about Karl's death,' I said.

'I've just finished speaking to the police. I don't have anything to add.'

'So you told them about the man who came to your door last night?'

Sybil stared at me. 'I don't know what you mean.'

'I think you do.' I pushed on. 'I saw him threatening you. Sybil, we can help, but you must tell us the truth.'

The woman seemed to crumble. She paled, sagging against the doorframe as if all the strength had gone from her body. Without answering, she merely nodded and motioned us in after her. The interior of her home was light and airy, with flower wallpaper and lacey curtains at the window.

We followed her into a kitchen that had an old-fashioned lemon yellow Laminex table in the centre and matching chairs. Sybil perched against the kitchen bench as we stood awkwardly in the middle of the room.

'There's not much I can tell you,' she said. 'You have to believe me, though, when I say I know nothing about Karl's death.'

'Who was that man I saw last night?' I asked.

'I can't tell you.'

'If you're in danger, you need to go to the police,' Kim said.

'No!' she said, terrified by the idea. 'Not the police!'

'What is it?' I insisted. 'What are you hiding?'

The woman burst into tears. I took a deep breath, not sure what to do. I inhaled again. Sniffed. Looked around. There was an odd scent in the air. The smell of chemicals.

'Sybil,' I said slowly. 'What's under this house?'

Tears streamed down her face. 'No!' she shrieked. 'I can't—I mean you mustn't—'

I marched back down the hallway to a door leading to the basement. Gripping the handle, I turned around to see Sybil silhouetted in the kitchen, her face stricken with resignation. Kim pushed past her as I opened the door.

A chemical stench wafted up from the basement.

Kim, Trixie, and I went down the stairs, the smell of ammonia catching at the back of my throat as I snapped on the lights. Fluorescents flickered to life, illuminating lab benches, Bunsen burners, cans of paint thinner, and a propane tank. A pile of empty plastic containers sat in a corner.

Kim stared. 'What is this?'

'It's a drug lab,' I said. 'Sybil is manufacturing crystal meth.'

Sybil appeared at the top of the stairs. 'I didn't want to...' she began. 'Our business was failing. If we lost the business, we'd lose our house. We had to do it. I thought it would end when Stewart died, but the man from Cape Carson kept coming here. He insists I keep manufacturing.'

'Was he the one threatening you?' I asked.

Sybil nodded.

'Who is it?' Kim asked.

'I don't know his real name,' Sybil said. 'He calls himself Barbie.'

'Barbie?'

'He supplies to someone in Melbourne,' she said. 'But he also deals through a pub in Cape Carson.'

Although there were three pubs in Cape Carson, only one was likely to have its own resident drug dealer. 'The Smuggler's Inn?' I asked.

'Yes. He's there most nights.'

'You need to go to the police,' Kim said.

'I can't do that,' Sybil said, terror in her eyes. 'Barbie said the gang would murder my brother. They know his address.'

A thought occurred to me. 'And Stewart?' I said. 'Is there any chance they killed him?'

At this, Sybil shook her head. 'No,' she said. 'They had no reason to. Stewart was always a better chemist than me, and he was prepared to follow their orders.'

'Regardless,' I said. 'You can't keep living like this. Crystal meth kills people. You've got to tell the authorities.'

'No! I can't!'

I understood her fear. If someone threatened my family, I'd do everything possible to keep them safe. But nothing would change if she didn't take a stand. 'Where does your brother live?' I asked.

'In Ballarat.'

It was a regional city west of Melbourne. 'The threat against him may not even be real,' I said. 'But you can warn him. Tell him to get out of town. I'll give you forty-eight hours to approach the police. If you don't, I'll do it—with or without your consent.'

'Sybil,' Kim said. 'Jamie Farrell was killed by crystal meth. Do you know anything about his death?'

'No,' Sybil sobbed. 'Jamie didn't get the stuff from us. I swear—we had nothing to do with Jamie's death.'

16

'You may find this hard to believe,' Grace Vickery said, 'but Karl and I were once in a relationship.'

It was hard to believe. Kim, Trixie, and I were sitting in Grace's living room, overlooking the bay. I glanced across at Kim, whose face was unreadable. We'd heard a lot of weird things over the last week. Hearing that this attractive woman had once been romantically attached to Karl was one more to add to the list.

'It happened not long after I first moved here.' Grace looked embarrassed. 'I know it sounds strange. He had such unusual beliefs.'

'We're not sure what his beliefs were,' Kim said tactfully.

'Karl saw himself as some kind of shaman. He thought he could communicate with the monster. He saw it once, you see. Or, at least, he thought he did. I think that changed him. He thought he had a connection with the creature.'

'What did he see?' I asked.

'He described it as a hazy shape in the water. After that, his whole life changed. He started delving into spiritual beliefs so that he could communicate with the monster.'

'Was he successful?'

'No. And I think that's what caused his decline. Karl wanted to see the creature again. It became an obsession.'

'Did anyone else know about your relationship?' Kim asked.

'No.'

'Why not?'

Grace gave a bitter laugh. 'You know how people are here,' she said. 'They talk behind your back. Say things. Sometimes they say awful things. I didn't want them talking about Karl and me together.'

'So what happened?' Kim asked. 'Why did you break up?'

Grace clenched her fists. 'I finally realised how silly it was. All his talk about the monster and animal spirits was just nonsense. I challenged him on his beliefs. We got into an argument, and I walked out. I tried speaking to him later, but he ignored me. So that was that: the end.'

I nodded. 'But it sounds like you have some resentment.'

'I don't like wasting time,' Grace said bitterly. 'Maybe it's because I've lost so many loved ones. I wasted time with Karl when I could have been enjoying life. So now I enjoy life as a single person.' She paused. 'Unlike Karl.'

It took me a moment to understand what she was saying. 'Are you saying Karl got into another relationship?'

'I'm not sure,' Grace said. 'I occasionally find it hard to sleep at night, so I sit at my bedroom window. I've seen Robyn go out late.'

'Robyn Pennington?'

Grace nodded. 'Ray goes off to events in Cape Carson all the time,' she said. 'It's the golf club, I think. Anyway, after he leaves, Robyn drives off.'

Robyn had said she liked to go on long drives.

I began. 'But to get to Karl's house unseen...'

'There's a stop-off point on Millicent Drive. You can park there and walk back through the dunes to the homes on that side.'

Could Robyn and Karl have been in a relationship? They seemed just as unlikely a couple as Grace and Karl. Robyn *could* have visited him last night. She could have even been the last person to see him alive. A lover's tiff could have led to his death. Stranger things have happened.

We thanked Grace for her time and were about to leave when I noticed the ceramic mouse sitting on the sideboard. I asked Grace where she'd bought it, and she said it was a giftware store in Cape Carson. She scribbled down the shop name with her left hand and gave me the page.

'It didn't cost a lot,' Grace said as she led us to the door.

'That's okay. My grandmother likes ceramic mice. It will suit her to a T.'

After thanking her, Kim, Trixie, and I headed back onto the path and started a slow walk along the side of the bay back towards Oxley street.

'So Robyn and Karl were in a relationship,' Kim said.

'*May* have been in a relationship. Grace wasn't certain.'

'Lots of people have killed each other over love. Look at Romeo and Juliet.'

I checked my watch.

It was late in the day now, and we hadn't eaten, and I was desperately missing my jumbo double-shot caramel lattes. Right now, I felt like driving back to Cape Carson to get one, but my attention was drawn to a vehicle pulling into the Farrell's driveway.

'We haven't spoken to them about Karl's death,' I said. 'They might have something to add.'

'They weren't very forthcoming before.'

'Maybe they will be this time. Now we're dealing with a murder.'

Jean gave us a friendly glance as we approached, but Robert's expression was *not you again*.

'We're here because of Karl,' I started.

Robert cut me off. 'You want to know what we thought of Karl? He was a weirdo like the other crazies in this town.

Anyway, we're busy, so please leave us alone.'

'I understand your anger.' I had to keep him talking—conversation leads to information—so I gambled with a white lie. 'I happen to know that Karl thought well of you both. He would have helped you if he could.'

Jean touched Robert's arm. 'Rob,' she said. 'Karl dropped off that food hamper after Jamie died.'

This was news to me.

Robert bit his lip. 'He was probably just being nosy,' he said. 'But...all right. Come in, but there's not much we can say.'

We followed them into the house and were soon in their living room. Trixie headed over to the hole in the floor. Panic appeared in Robert's face.

'Come away from there!' he said.

I called Trixie away.

Now that's odd, I thought.

'We should tell Kim and Rosie about last night,' Jean said.

He was sullen. 'Nothing happened last night.'

'Robert,' she persevered.

He relented. 'After you came to see me, I thought back on Karl's behaviour. He's always been strange and I thought the police should have pushed him further about Jamie's death. Anyway, I went to see him last night. Or I tried to. It was late. I'd had a few drinks. Jean told me not to go, but I did anyway.'

'What time was this?'

'Sometime after midnight. Maybe half past. I was almost at his place when I heard arguing.'

'From Karl's place?'

Robert nodded. 'It was hard to make out, but I definitely heard Karl say the words *pure evil*.'

I shuddered. If there were a serial killer in Port Logan, that would be a good way to describe them. 'Were you able to make out the other voice?'

'No.'

'Not even if it was male or female?'

'Sorry. I could hardly make out Karl's voice. I stood there for a while and was about to leave when I heard a gunshot.' He stopped. 'It scared me. I was standing out on the path in full view of his house. I expected the person who fired the gun to come out and shoot me too.'

'What did you do?' Kim asked.

'Well, like I said, at first I was frozen like a rabbit. I must have been there for a good minute or two. Then I heard a sound from the building, so I dived into the nearest bushes. It was a couple of seconds later that the front door opened, and someone came down the steps.'

'Did you see who it was?'

'No. They wore a hood and rain jacket.'

'Colour?'

'Dark. Maybe dark green.'

It's the same person the others described.

'Okay,' I said, thoughtfully. 'Then what?'

'They went in the direction of East Head.'

'You're sure? It wasn't the other way?'

'No. It was definitely that way.'

'What did you do then?'

'What do you think I did?' He swallowed. 'I ran. I haven't run like that since I was a kid. I raced home, slammed the door behind me, and locked it.'

'You didn't ring the police?' Kim said.

Jean spoke up. 'After what happened to Jamie?' she said. Her eyes darted to the hole in the floor. 'The police never said it, but they grilled us like we were suspects. Like they thought we'd killed Jamie. They'd think we were involved in Karl's death.'

'You need to speak to them,' Kim said.

Robert resolutely shook his head. 'No way.'

I didn't want to argue. These people had been through enough already. After thanking them for their time, Kim and I returned to the street. It was afternoon now, I felt exhausted, and my head had begun to ache again.

'What's going on with that hole in the floor?' Kim asked.

'You noticed that too? I have no idea.'

'They're hiding something—but what?'

It was a complete mystery and one we couldn't solve right now.

'So, what's our next step?' Kim asked.

'Now we're heading to Sandy's Diner, and I'm having an enormous caramel latte.'

'Jumbo sized?' Kim asked.

'Bucket sized,' I said. 'And even that might not be big enough!'

17

As it turned out, our favourite diner didn't do bucket sized caramel lattes, but Sandy thought there could be a market for it.

'It would be a special,' she said, placing our coffees down. 'I'd make it for anyone investigating murders.'

'Or library cataloguing,' Kim added. 'Some miscellaneous items are *really* hard to catalogue.'

We sipped our coffee, looking out at the bay from the front window at Sandy's.

It was mid-afternoon, and Trixie was ensconced in front with a bowl of water nearby. On the beach, kids were feeding seagulls. A little boat was rounding the breakwater and heading for the wharf. An elderly couple walked hand in hand in the direction of the lighthouse.

It's good to be home, I thought.

The world of Port Logan was a strange one and made all the weirder by the death of Karl Hoffman.

'Okay, Kim,' I said. 'Let's look at what we've got.'

'Do we have to? Can't I just go back to the library and shelve books for the rest of my life?'

'And let a serial killer run loose?'

'Rosie,' Kim said. 'You know I only love scary things when I can turn them off with a remote control. When they're real, I'd rather run in the opposite direction.'

'We've already made headway. We can't stop now.'

'All right,' Kim groaned. 'If we must.'

'Great,' I said, ignoring Kim's reluctance. 'Let's look at what we've got. The first person killed was Florence Teale. She came to visit her friend Grace and was in Port Logan for all of five minutes before she was run over. The car that ran her over was seen by Iris, who followed it into the dunes. She saw the killer set the vehicle alight before escaping.'

'This was the mysterious Raincoat Killer,' Kim said, brightening. 'Hey, the *Raincoat Killer*! What a great name.'

'Yes. How entertaining it is to invent monikers for serial killers.'

'You're no fun.'

'I know,' I said, pausing. 'Now, we've only got Iris's word that she saw the killer.'

'True. But the killer has also been ID'd by Robert and Philip.'

'So that means the Raincoat Killer is real. That's a step forward. The next death was Jamie Farrell, who died from crystal meth. We know that Sybil and Stewart have been cooking meth in their basement, although Sybil swears it didn't come from them.'

'So there could be a connection.'

'Yep. And then the next death was Cynthia Shepherd, who supposedly fell onto her own knife.'

'Which has got to be the most unlikely accident in human history,' Kim said. 'It's amazing that anyone believed it in the first place. Again, no one saw Raincoat on that occasion.' She frowned. 'So who was next?'

'Stewart Bard.'

'No one saw Raincoat that time either.'

'Although we did find a mark on the rock where it looked like it had been loosened.' I stopped. 'You know, we haven't checked to see if there was a piece of knotted rope at those crime scenes. There could be one where Stewart died, as well as where Cynthia was killed.'

'Cynthia was killed on a boat. Knots would be everywhere.'

'True, but that type of rope is quite distinctive. Where we did find rope was back at Florence, Karl and Jamie's crime scenes.' I took a long sip of my coffee. 'Raincoat has been seen by Robert, Philip, and Iris. Surely that means Raincoat must be either Ray, Robyn, Jean, or Grace.'

'Maybe,' Kim said. 'But there's a big problem with your

theory. We don't know if any of them are telling the truth. Any of them could be Raincoat and lying about seeing the killer.'

Kim was right. It was all well and good that these people all claimed to have seen the killer, but it really meant nothing. Any of them could have been the killer and lied to cover their tracks.

'Oh dear,' I said. 'This makes my head ache.'

'A good night's sleep will fix you up, except the council meeting's on.'

'I know.' I glanced at my watch. 'How are you feeling about your speech?'

'Nervous. Can't you give it instead?'

'No,' I said. 'And you'll be fine.'

We finished our coffees, collected Trixie, and jumped in my jeep.

A few minutes later, we pulled up in front of the council chambers. The building was a series of interconnecting, jar-shaped concrete offices next to the public library. Although this was still closed for renovations, the council was very much open. There were more cars parked out the front than I'd ever seen before.

'Wow,' I said. 'Looks like it's going to be quite an event.'

The council chambers were located on the ground floor past the front desk. So many people had turned up for the meeting that they spilled into the hallway.

It was an amazing cross-section of the Cape Carson community: surfers who'd brought their boards, bikers dressed in their leather gear, retirees with wheely walkers, mums and dads, kids, and shop owners. There were lots of dogs too, and Wanda Gibson had even turned up with her cat, Bastet. Most of the crowd, I knew by sight or by name.

Nan, Dave, Amanda, and Tom were squeezed together on the other side of the room. I wanted to join them, but first I had to chat to Harry, who was seated near the circular bench where the councillors were seated.

I gave him a wave and approached.

'There's already been some discussion,' Harry explained. 'The councillors called a recess because so many people have turned up to speak about the boatshed. It doesn't look like they expected such a big turnout.'

'I don't think anyone did.'

I cast my eyes over the crowd again. A familiar face stuck out immediately, and I manoeuvred over to him. 'Keith,' I said. 'Nice to see you here.'

He pushed back his blonde hair as his green eyes focused on mine. 'Wouldn't miss this for the world,' he said. 'You know, *power to the people* and all that. How do you think the council will vote?'

'I'm not sure.'

Cape Carson had nine elected council representatives, including the mayor and deputy mayor. These included members from the major political parties as well as more than a few independents. The result was a ragtag bunch of people with varying skills who spent most of their time arguing about issues they didn't understand very well. I'd attended dozens of these meetings over the years, and it seemed getting into public office depended on how many friends you had at the local bowling club.

'They're an odd bunch,' I said. 'Seeing them at work has never inspired me to get into public office.'

'Politics is a dirty game,' Keith said, his face darkening. 'Business can be a dirty game too.'

'You never know how things will turn out when money's concerned.'

He nodded glumly. 'No matter what happens,' he said, 'try not to be too disappointed. Some things are simply out of our control.'

Keith looked so unhappy that I felt like hugging him.

Instead, I gave his arm a squeeze, and he smiled sadly. Nan waved frantically from the other side of the room. Excusing myself, I edged over to her.

'Glad you could make it,' Nan said. 'We need all the moral support we can get.'

'Nan, do I need to remind you that I'm an unbiased—'

'Member of the media? Ha! Good luck with that!'

I turned to Amanda and Tom. 'So Nan talked you into coming?'

'We had no choice,' Tom said, raising an eyebrow. 'Nan threatened to block us in with Dave's car.'

'Nan!' I admonished her.

'Someone's got to take a stand.'

Dave gave a wry smile. 'I just wish she wouldn't use my car!'

It was nice to see that he and Nan were back on speaking terms. There was a stirring at the entrance to the council chambers, and the councillors filed in. The most imposing one was Mayor Lynch, who was always reminiscent of a dry storm: lots of bluster with few results.

She brought the meeting to order with a banging of the gavel. 'A big welcome to everyone who has just joined us,' the mayor began. 'There's obviously been a lot of discussion about the next development application.'

There was a general rumble of agreement in the crowd.

'The relevant planning reports have been submitted to council. These were found to comply with council guidelines. Additionally, 221 submissions were received from the public, many of which opposed the development.'

One of the councillors asked a question. 'What proportion of submissions were in favour?' he asked. 'And how many against?'

The mayor referred to her notes. 'Those opposing were 174,

and those in favour numbered 29. Those not stating a definite position made up the remaining.'

'Seems an overwhelming majority oppose the development,' another councillor commented.

This was met with a general chorus of *yes* in the crowd.

'We still need to hear verbal submissions,' Mayor Lynch said. 'I know that for many here this evening, this is their first time at council, and I welcome you. As well as taking written submissions into account, the long-established protocol of Cape Carson council is to listen to two verbal submissions from the public, each of three minutes duration. This is to ensure that the council meeting doesn't go for a week. Will the clerk now read the name of the first speaker?'

The first name to be read was that of Giuseppe Costa. The businessman took to the microphone, straightened his tie, and began.

'Lady Mayor, councillors and—last, but not least—the wonderful people of Cape Carson,' he began. 'I've been a resident of this town my entire life. It's been good to me, my wife, my neighbours and my friends. There are many things to appreciate about this town: the environment, people and lifestyle.

'Of course, none of us could live here without the businesses that support our community. The Percy Street precinct, that we so often take for granted, is the hub of our community. If it didn't exist, then we simply could not live in this great town. We would be forced to live elsewhere.

'Business is an essential part of Cape Carson and I wonder if you know how many have gone belly-up in the last year? The number is twelve, if you're wondering. Twelve people and their families who took the plunge to try to make a living. They deserve respect for their courage and the sacrifices they made to try to make their aspirational dreams come true.

'The old boatshed on the foreshore can be a great business. It doesn't have that capability right now. It's an ugly stain on our beautiful foreshore. Turning it into a fish and chip shop will encourage more people to come to Cape Carson. It will provide employment. The money that comes into the local economy will filter through to the other businesses and help them too. The development application that I've submitted is within the council guidelines. The building is not of heritage value. It's a liability to this town rather than an asset.

'I urge the council to approve this development. This business will help the entire town. More importantly, it will help, not just this generation, but generations to come. Thank you.'

Giuseppe Costa sat back down beside his wife.

He didn't write that speech, I thought. *The man can barely write a coherent sentence, let alone a speech!*

As the crowd gave a small round of applause, I glanced across at Giuseppe's wife, Sharon. She took his hand and gave him a small smile. *Sharon was probably the author.* It seemed unfair, but there wasn't a law stating that people had to write their own submissions.

Next, it was Kim who got up to speak.

'Lady Mayor, councillors, and people of Cape Carson.' The room fell to silence as she spoke. 'We've just heard an eloquent presentation telling us why the old boatshed on the water's edge should be torn down, and a new building erected. Now I will tell you why that is a terrible idea.

'That boatshed isn't covered under heritage protection laws, but it is part of our heritage. It's one of the oldest buildings in Cape Carson. It was built by shipwright John Carr. If you think the name is familiar, he was the son of Edward Carr, Cape Carson's first lighthouse keeper. The tiny shack was used as the first fisherman's co-op, a place that allowed people to prepare their catches for sale.

'The early town of Cape Carson was built on the fishing trade, and that continues to this day. Now, of course, the new co-op building attached to the wharf functions as the processing centre. The old building has sat deserted for years.

'On one point, I'll agree with Giuseppe Costa. The time has come for the boatshed to be revitalised, but it must be done in such a way that it complements our heritage. Too much of Cape Carson has already been lost to development. Once a building is destroyed, it is lost forever. It is lost to the people of today and to future generations. The boatshed has been there for over a hundred years. This is our chance to act decisively to help it survive for a hundred more.

'All around Australia, there are a million places like Cape Carson. It's the unique things about Cape Carson that make it precious. It's our point of difference. Another faceless, name-less, and—frankly—ugly building on our foreshore won't stay in people's memories. A renovated, revitalised, and thriving hundred-year-old boatshed can be a centrepiece of which this town can be proud.

'Lady Mayor and councillors, you can clearly see how many people here tonight oppose this development.' The crowd gave a general clap in agreement. 'I urge you to listen to the people of Cape Carson, listen to the 174 submissions opposing the development, and listen to future generations who want the boatshed saved!'

As Kim finished, there was a roar of approval. People leaped to their feet and clapped wildly. Surfers hammered on their surfboards. Dogs barked. Wanda's cat, Bastet, sat on her shoulder and yowled. I exchanged glances with Keith, whose face was filled with admiration.

I felt a warm glow. It was nice to see that he was so concerned about the area, despite not being a local resident.

Once the crowd had settled down, the Mayor thanked everyone for attending the council meeting.

'This has been a meeting like no other in recent memory,' she said. 'Most of these meetings, we're lucky if half a dozen people turn up. We will now put it to a vote, and I ask everyone to remain seated and quiet until the vote has completed.' She referred to the pages in her hand. 'We will now put development application DA34872-B to the vote. Will all those in favour of the application please raise their hands?'

18

'To the boatshed!' I cried.

'The boatshed!' everyone else chorused.

We were sitting inside Sandy's Diner the next morning. Not only were members of my family cramming the table, but the place was so packed that it felt like half the town had turned up to celebrate the victory. Word had gotten around that Sandy's was the place to celebrate.

'And to Kim!' I added.

Kim turned red as everyone cheered her. Someone called out *Mayor Kim,* and half the diner was filled with voices chanting the slogan. This made her even more embarrassed.

'This is crazy!' she said. 'All I did was make a speech!'

'Don't be silly,' Nan said. 'It was a great speech and made all the difference.'

Amanda leaned close. 'Giuseppe Costa didn't look pleased.'

'No,' I agreed. 'He didn't.'

I'd expected him to look furious; he had a notoriously bad

temper. Instead, a grim look had crossed his face, and he had left quietly with Sharon soon after the meeting concluded. Maybe he'd known all along that the development wouldn't succeed. It was a tactic often used by developers to ask for more than they could get, and that way, they got exactly what they wanted.

Dave was squeezed in beside Nan in the booth. 'What'll happen now?' he asked. 'Does this mean the boatshed is saved?'

'Yes and no,' Kim said. 'Giuseppe won't put in the same development application. That would be a complete waste of time. He might propose a smaller building or something else.'

Tom leaned in. 'His best shot is to simply renovate the building,' he said. 'From last night, that's clearly what the council would approve.'

'I suppose time will tell,' I said.

Nothing happened too quickly in Cape Carson. That was probably another reason why we liked it so much. I glanced at my watch. I'd stayed at my place last night, but Kim and I had a few jobs to do before heading back to Port Logan. We finished our coffees, ordered more takeaways, and we headed outside where I'd left Trixie.

A now-familiar person was passing by.

'Hello ladies,' Keith said. 'Still partying? I hope you got some sleep.'

'I'm afraid my days of all-night parties are over,' I said with a grin. 'Although I was up till almost midnight.'

'Then you did better than me. I was out like a light by eleven.' He glanced at his watch. 'Sorry, got to run. I've got a business meeting to attend.'

We wished him a good day and headed to my jeep. As we climbed in, Kim turned to me. 'He seems nice,' she said. 'Not as nice as Todd, though.'

'You don't think?'

Kim fixed her gaze on me. 'Okay,' she said. 'I can see he's handsome, but don't fall for a pretty face. Todd's a reliable guy.'

'And Keith isn't?'

'What do you know about him?'

I held up my hands in surrender. 'Fair enough,' I said. 'I promise not to marry Keith without your permission. Now let's get going.'

Trixie settled into the back seat and peered out the window as we headed down the street to Casey's Supermarket. It only took a few minutes. Owned by a big jolly guy named Stan Gilstrap, Casey's ran like clockwork.

Despite being almost sixty, Stan still worked every day except Mondays and kept the place completely stocked and clean. We arrived to find him in the tinned food aisle, restocking soup cans.

'Hello ladies,' he said. 'You interested in soup? On special this week? Three for the price of two?'

'Tomato soup is one of my favourites,' I confirmed, 'but we need some help with something.'

I explained that we wanted to review his video footage for the last forty-eight hours. 'I'm doing some research.'

Stan smiled, scratching his chin. 'Research or investigating?'

'A bit of both,' Kim said.

'For anyone else, I'd say no,' Stan said. 'But because you're both so beautiful, the answer is yes.'

Laughing, we followed him to a cramped room where he showed us his security system. It comprised a single television screen split into six views of different parts of the shop.

'Were you looking for anyone in particular?' he asked.

'Maybe,' I said. 'I have to protect my source.'

'I have to protect my sauces too. Especially BBQ.'

Stan was renowned for his bad jokes. He pointed to the camera showing the checkout. 'This shows everyone coming and going,' he said. 'You can pick the day and time and fast forward through. It's not fun viewing. I've had to sit through days of footage trying to find shoplifters.'

'Do you catch them in the end?'

He rolled his eyes. 'Usually,' he said. 'You wouldn't believe what people try. Last week, I caught a guy trying to stuff a cooked chicken down the front of his pants.'

'Your food is just way too good,' I said.

'I know,' Stan laughed. 'As long as people pay, they can have it!'

Thanking him, Kim and I settled down at the television monitor with Trixie at our feet.

'I'm guessing we're looking for Philip?' Kim said.

'You got it. Philip said he came here the night Karl was murdered and bought flowers.'

'And you don't think he did?'

'We'll see.'

The following two hours passed slowly in the tiny room as Kim and I scoured the video footage. Not only did we examine the film from the checkout, but also the flower stand, just in case Philip had stolen the plants rather than pay for them. In the end, we both sat back and stretched.

'Well,' I said. 'That settles it. Philip didn't buy his flowers here.'

'Maybe he made a mistake? He could have gotten them from somewhere else.'

'Where Kim? The florist closes at five. This is the only late opening place that sells cut flowers.'

'And this is important because...'

'Just a theory,' I said mysteriously. 'Now, let's see if I'm right.'

We returned to my jeep and drove back to Port Logan. Parking in Nola and Monica's driveway, we'd just gotten out of the car when I saw Philip disappearing around the headland.

We briskly walked along the path and soon caught up with him.

'On a morning walk?' he asked.

'No,' I said. 'I needed to talk to you about gerberas.'

'Gerberas?'

'Specifically, the ones on your kitchen window.'

He frowned. 'I told you they came from the supermarket—'

'That's a lie,' I interrupted. 'Kim and I just spent two hours searching the supermarket's security footage. Do you want to tell us the truth?'

He stared at us in silence.

'Those flowers are from Robyn's garden,' I said. 'Aren't they? They're lovely plants. I remember looking at them the first day we arrived. But that's strange, isn't it? Why would she give you flowers? And when? I've never seen you together.'

'I...well...she's a friend...'

'Philip.' I lowered my voice. 'You and Robyn are having an affair, and it shouldn't be happening, but it is. The most important thing now is for you to admit it so you can be ruled out as a suspect.'

He clenched his jaw and peered out at the shifting ocean. 'I didn't mean for it to happen,' he said, finally. 'I'm not that kind of man, and Robyn is a good woman.' He clenched his fists. 'But her husband is an idiot! He treats her like furniture.'

'How long has this been going on?'

He shrugged. 'A year.'

'And Ray hasn't noticed?' Kim asked.

'The only thing he sees is his own ego,' Philip said. 'Ray would never believe that his wife would have an affair.'

I frowned. 'But if Robyn goes out at all hours—'

'Ray thinks she just likes to drive.' He paused. 'Well, she does like to drive—to where we meet up in the dunes.'

'And Ray suspects nothing?'

'Ray is constantly having affairs,' Philip said, shaking his head. 'Women fall for him before realising he's a complete narcissist.'

We asked Philip if he knew anything else about who could have killed Karl.

'No,' he said. 'But Ray is out most evenings too. Although he tells Robyn that he goes fishing, he rarely comes back with any fish.'

'Really? But he leaves in his boat?'

Philip nodded.

We thanked him for his time and strolled back towards Nola and Monica's place.

'It seems everyone in this place has a double life,' Kim said, thoughtfully.

'The rumours about Nola and Monica being vampires

could be true.'

'Do you think so? But we've seen them in daylight—'

'You idiot!' I said, punching Kim's arm. 'Of course, they're not vampires! But I think we need to work out where Ray's going.'

Back in Nola and Monica's basement unit, I sat down and typed up my notes about the case while Kim settled down to read for the day. All the while, we kept an eye on Ray's home. It wasn't until evening that his front door eased open, and Ray appeared. He said something to Robyn before heading for the jetty.

'He's wearing an anorak,' Kim said. 'But it's not dark green.'

'He could own more than one,' I said.

We watched Ray get into his boat and cast off.

'Come on,' I said. 'Let's get moving.' He pulled away from the jetty as Kim and I piled into my jeep with Trixie. Keeping Ray's boat in sight, we drove up the hill. Slowing at the top, I dragged a pair of binoculars from my glove compartment and handed them to Kim. 'We should be able to keep sight of him if he heads east towards Cape Carson.'

'And if he doesn't?'

'Then we're in trouble.'

'He's heading straight out to sea,' Kim said, peering through the binoculars. 'No. Wait a minute. He *is* heading east.'

'Fantastic!'

I accelerated down Millicent Drive. The night had turned cold, and Ray's boat was a tiny dot of light in the ocean. Kim kept the binoculars trained on him while I watched the road. Twenty minutes later, we pulled into Cape Carson at the same time as his boat came around the breakwater and into the bay.

We stopped in the beachside car park as he left his boat. Ducking behind some rubbish bins, we watched as he strode past us. Gone was the anorak, replaced by a sports jacket and dark trousers.

'Where did he get those from?' Kim asked.

'He must keep them on the boat.'

We trailed behind as Ray Pennington made his way through town. It only took him a few minutes to reach his destination.

'The RSL club?' Kim said. 'What's he doing here?'

'Meeting someone,' I suggested. 'Or gambling. That place is wall-to-wall with poker machines.'

Tying Trixie up out the front, we entered, keeping a discrete distance behind as Ray walked through the poker machine saloon. I expected him to stop there. Instead, he continued on to one of the lounges beyond.

'Where's he going?' Kim hissed.

I didn't answer. We followed Ray into one of the entertainment showrooms. The dimly lit space had a small bar near the entrance and seating surrounding a semi-circular stage at the other end. The place was full of people, mostly older, retired folk. I peered about the gloomy interior. There was no sign of Ray.

'Where's he gone?' I asked.

An emcee got onto the stage and grabbed the microphone. 'Welcome to another night of local talent,' he said. 'I'm Johnny Barrister, and I'm your host with the most. We've got a big evening planned with lots of music and song.'

There was a scattering of applause. Kim and I took refuge in the shadowy seating at the back.

'One of our regulars is up first,' Johnny continued. 'A man you all know and love with a hit from the King himself.'

In the front row, a very drunk woman raised her glass and yelled out. 'I love Elvis!'

'We all do, luv.'

'I'll be his queen.'

'Right you are. Now let's have a round of applause for our first act of the evening, Bruno Swagger!'

The singer, a moustached man, dressed like Elvis in a white diamante studded jumpsuit, took to the stage as the first notes of *Burning Love* echoed from the tinny sound system. He started singing as my eyes swept the audience. *Ray's got to be here somewhere.* He must come for entertainment. Or maybe to meet someone. Probably a woman.

I peered more closely at a man in the front row.

Is that him?

'Rosie,' Kim said.

'Can you see him?'

Kim nudged me. She was staring at Bruno. Following her gaze, I did a double-take. Bruno wore a handlebar moustache and had slicked-back hair. Despite this, now that I looked more closely, the face below the moustache was one I recognised.

'You've got to be kidding,' I said.

'Ray is Elvis,' Kim said. 'I mean...Bruno is Elvis...no, I mean...'

'I know what you mean.'

I stared at him, fascinated. There was no denying it. Ray may have been one of the most egotistical men I'd ever met, but he made for a decent Elvis. In addition to being able to carry a tune, he had the dance and waist movements down to a T.

The man finished his song, thanked the emcee, and left the stage. Kim and I exchanged glances.

'Well,' I said. 'I didn't see that coming.'

'I know. He's a terrible painter but a reasonable singer.'

We settled back to enjoy the evening. Several people got up to perform, and the talent ranged from terrible to bearable. Ray got up twice more to perform Elvis hits. Each time, the crowd gave him rousing applause. Or what passed for rousing in this place.

The show ended just after nine o'clock, and a good thing too. I was ready to get moving. Just as I got up, though, Kim grabbed my arm.

'Look!' she hissed.

Ray had appeared from stage left wearing his civvies. He had sat down at a front table where a woman we didn't recognise arrowed over to sit beside him. She leaned over and kissed him on the lips.

'What on Earth—' I started.

'Right,' Kim said. 'A secret Elvis impersonator *and* having an affair.'

'Talk about a double life. Or is that a triple life?'

The two got up and disappeared through a side door.

'What now?' Kim asked. 'Back to Port Logan?'

'I wish. There's somewhere else we need to check out.'

Despite being exhausted, there was still another lead I needed to follow.

Kim and I drove to the Smuggler's Inn. I'd been here before at night, and it was always the same: a cross between the Mos Eisley cantina from Star Wars and a full-scale prison riot. Every lowlife and desperado from here to Melbourne seemed to come here after dark. Some guys were wrestling on the floor in a corner. Two women were playing a drinking game at a table. One knocked back a shot of hard liquor, and gave her companion a triumphant grin before toppling sideways off her chair. A couple was making out at the bar.

'Goodness,' Kim said. 'This is amazing.'

'Never been here before?'

'Once when I was at high school. A friend dared me to enter. I lasted ten seconds before I turned and ran.' She glanced around. 'And that was during the day.'

We elbowed our way through the crowd as a few of the men gave us appraising glances. I was taller than most men, which meant I stood out like a sore thumb, so I tried to stoop a little. It had gotten me through six years of high school; surely, it would work now.

'What'll it be?' the barman asked. He was a middle-aged guy with a scruffy brown beard and a t-shirt that read *KISS Lives Forever*. 'Kim Chen? Is that you?'

'Earl Ross?'

'It *is* you. How have you been?'

'Great.' She stared at him, not sure how to proceed. 'What are you up to these days?'

'Still working on my music,' Earl said, scratching under his chin. 'Just started a new band: Zombies of Death. We do retro-gothic-underground punk.'

'Oh.'

'It's like the Sex Pistols, but cooler.' He studied Kim's face and the bare ring finger on her left hand. 'Not married?'

'No...yes...I mean, not at the moment.' Kim looked at me helplessly before blurting, 'I'm a librarian.'

I wasn't sure that had anything to do with marriage. 'Two

glasses of Coke,' I ordered. 'Not too much ice, please.'

'Won't be any ice,' Earl grinned, showing a row of missing top teeth. 'Ice machine's broken.'

Why does that not surprise me?

'What happened to your teeth?' Kim asked as he made our drinks.

'I was coasting down Barrack Hill on a shopping trolley when one of the wheels came off. Smashed face-first into the road. Should have sued the supermarket. Those trollies are a menace.'

Yes, Kim and I agreed silently. Those shopping trollies should really carry a warning sign about using them on public roads. We grabbed our drinks and angled for the shadows at the back of the pub.

'How strange,' Kim said. 'At high school, Earl was voted most likely to become a successful musician.'

'He might still do that.'

'Maybe. But he'll need to get his teeth fixed.'

It would help. I glanced about, my eyes searching the gloom as a song by John Cougar Mellencamp started playing. Now we had to find the man known as Barbie. It couldn't be his real name. Only a drunk would name their son Barbie. It ranked as one of my all-time least favourite names, along with Adolf, Osama, and Gaylord.

'We need to ask around to see if anyone knows him,' I said.

'We can pretend to be buying drugs.'

'Leave it to me. There's a look people give each other when they're trying to score drugs. It's sort of a wink and a nod.'

My knowledge of buying drugs was precisely zero. I'd tried marijuana once when I was a teenager and threw up. 'Okay,' I said uncertainly.

'I had a boyfriend who was a drug addict.'

'Oh?'

'Yep,' Kim continued, glumly. 'Another loser. He's in jail now for robbery. Anyway, let me try this. I saw Jacko do this all the time.'

'I don't think—'

Kim caught the eye of a nearby male and gave a half-wink as she nodded, throwing in a grin for good measure.

The overall effect was one of someone either in a state of extreme intoxication or in need of a hospital. Or both. The man saw her, frowned, and moved away.

'Oh dear,' Kim said. 'That didn't seem to work.'

'We've already got an in. Your friend Earl probably knows every lowlife from here to Melbourne. I'll ask him.'

Leaving Kim in the shadows, I returned to the bar.

'Barbie?' Earl said. 'He's out the back in the pool room.'

'What's he look like?'

'Denim jacket with no sleeves.' Earl leaned close. 'Be careful. It can get rough out there.'

Rougher than this?

I pushed back through the crowd. In the short time I'd been away, Kim had met up with two beefy, biker dudes. One wore an eyepatch while the other's left hand had been replaced by a hook.

'This is Trash and—' Kim stopped. 'What did you say your name is?'

'Crank,' the hook-handed man said. 'Kimmy here was just saying how much she'd like to go for a ride.'

'Sorry, guys,' I said. 'We're meeting someone. Catch you later.'

Grabbing her arm, I shoved her in the direction of the pool room. 'Boy,' I said. 'You really know how to pick them. Those guys looked like bad news.'

'Crank I've never met,' Kim said, 'but I went to school with Trash years ago.'

'Really?'

'Back then, he was Simon.'

'Should have stuck with it.'

The pool room was a double chamber joined by an archway. Guys hung about playing pool. Some looked like they belonged to the same biker gang as Trash and Crank. A few others were dishevelled hippies with long, grey hair and beards, and t-shirts faded to pastel shades of nothing. They looked like surfer dudes who had caught the wave on that endless summer many years ago and had gotten stuck in the shallows.

The pool room was as dimly lit as the rest of the pub. I peered about the gloom looking for someone who could be a drug dealer.

'Which one do you think is Barbie?' Kim murmured.

'No idea. They all look like drug dealers to me.'

Then one of the bikers put down his cue stick and yelled out.

'Hey, Barbie!' he said. 'Best of three?'

A figure emerged from the other room and snatched up a pool stick.

'Sure,' Nico said. 'Why not?'

19

'That boy is in a whole world of trouble,' Nan said, slamming down her coffee cup. 'I knew he was no good from the day I met him.'

I was sitting in the kitchen with Nan and Amanda the next day. They had remained silent until I finished telling them what Kim and I had discovered.

'Nan,' I said patiently. 'I seem to recall that you liked both George and Nico in the beginning.'

'That's not quite true. I always liked George because he's a Geelong Cat's supporter.' The football club was a lifelong passion for her. 'But I always had my doubts about Nico. He barracked for Carlton, and I knew he was no good.'

'Well,' I said. 'Doubt no longer.'

'What I don't understand is why he's going under the nick-name of Barbie.'

'That stumped me too, at first,' I said. 'It's his hair. He has it in a ponytail.'

'He gives Barbie a bad name.'

Amanda spoke up. 'Mum,' she said. 'What will happen to Nico if you tell the cops?'

I thought. 'I don't know,' I said. 'He'll go to jail. For how long, I'm not sure, but he's dealing in a serious drug, and in large quantities by the look of it. And he's threatening Sybil.'

'Dad will be devastated.'

'I don't want to hurt your Dad. I really don't, but this can't be allowed to go on.'

'Can't you just tell Nico to stop?'

I hesitated. 'Amanda, we can't know for sure that it's just Nico.'

She stared at me. 'You don't mean that Dad's involved?' she said. 'He would never do such a thing!'

I wasn't so sure about that. While George had never been a criminal, he had skirted the law over the years. If he could get away with safely running a red light in a remote location, he'd do it. Likewise, if George found money on the street, he wouldn't go to any great trouble trying to track down the owner.

'I don't know what his involvement is,' I said. 'I've just met his new girlfriend. She seems nice. It's hard to believe she'd want anything to do with this.'

Nan cut in. 'Rosie,' she said. 'Just a reminder: your boyfriend is a policeman.'

'Todd's not my boyfriend,' I said for the millionth time. 'And I know what Todd will do. He'll arrest Nico without thinking twice.' Sybil would also get charged, and she'd already told me that Nico had threatened to harm her brother. This was a horrible situation, a lose-lose all around. 'I told Sybil that I'd give her forty-eight hours to do the right thing. Then I'll go to the cops.'

'Mum,' Amanda said, frowning. 'She could already be in danger. People on drugs are unpredictable.'

I remembered how Nico had been at George's barbeque. How he'd tried to pick me up and failed. He hadn't joined us in playing charades, instead deciding to go out straight after eating.

'You're right,' I said. 'I'll speak with Sybil.'

Leaving Trixie with Nan, I jumped in my jeep and was soon back at the garden centre. The gates were open, and the woman had just finished serving an elderly customer. Waiting until the customer had gone, I strolled into the office and told Sybil we needed to have a conversation.

'If it's about what's going on at my house,' Sybil said, 'then I can't talk about it.'

'We *must* talk about it.' I explained that the man she knew as Barbie was Nico, my ex-brother-in-law. 'I'm sorry all of this has gone so pear-shaped, but there's no getting away from the fact that Nico is threatening you. You've got to go to the police. Things will only get worse. It's not only the drug Nico's addicted to. It's the money. You're supplying a steady stream of big dollars to him. This will go on forever.'

Sybil looked ready to burst into tears. 'You can't betray my trust,' she said. 'You said I could have forty-eight hours.'

'And you do,' I said. 'I'm saying this as a friend. You're in danger if you keep doing this.' I hesitated, thinking. 'We also have to consider the possibility that Nico is involved in Karl Hoffman's death.'

Sybil's jaw dropped. 'That's impossible!'

'It's very unlikely,' I hastened to add. Even I didn't believe it. Nico had no reason to kill Karl. 'But he's a criminal dealing with some unsavoury characters.' I thought of how strange he had been the night of the barbeque. It made more sense now I knew he was on hard drugs. 'If you keep doing what you're doing, you'll keep getting the same result. If you speak to the police of your own volition, I'm sure they'll be more lenient. You'll never need to be under Nico's control again.'

'But Rosie, it means I'll lose everything. My home. The garden centre. My reputation. I'll go to jail.'

'You might not go to jail if you approach the police yourself,' I said.

I wasn't sure about this.

Nor was I convinced that Jamie Farrell's death wasn't connected to them. It seemed like a massive coincidence that Jamie had died from the same drug they were manufacturing in their lab.

The woman took a deep breath. 'Let me think about it,' she said. 'This is too big a decision for me to make right now.'

'I've already given you time.'

'Please, Rosie,' she said. 'You said forty-eight hours.'

I hesitated. 'And half of that time has gone,' I said. 'I'm going to the police tomorrow—with or without you.'

Sybil nodded. I made my way to my jeep and drove off. *She's got to come to her senses. It's the best way forward.* Driving into town, I pulled over and called Todd to ask about Karl's death.

'I'm glad you rang,' Todd said. 'We're still investigating, but I wanted to thank you for that tip about the knots at the crime scenes.'

'So you think a serial killer's at work?'

'Can we speak off the record?'

'Absolutely.'

'The crimes seem to be linked. There have been several deaths, and it seems like too much of a coincidence that the same knotted rope was at four of the crime scenes.'

'Four?'

'We checked the coastal path where Stewart Bard died. A knot was tied to the old fence that used to run along there.'

'What about Cynthia's boat?'

'We located her boat, *Great Expectations*. The new owners

had it in drydock for a total restoration, so it's been stripped. If there were a knot on board, it's long gone.' He paused. 'By the way, Rosie, I should mention that the media have contacted me from Melbourne.'

So the Melbourne media is already onto this, I thought. The Cape Carson Gazette was going to print tonight, and Harry would have my head if we weren't taking the lead on this story.

'What have you told them?' I asked.

'Not much. We're releasing a press release shortly.'

'Can you email it to me?'

He said he would. Hanging up, I drove into town, stopping outside the Gazette. As I bustled in through the front door, Harry's voice rang out from his office.

'Is that the female reporter who used to work here?' he yelled.

I leaned into his office. 'You did tell me to follow up on the Port Logan monster.'

'That doesn't mean going AWOL for days without keeping me updated,' he said, annoyed. 'I've got a double page to fill, and all Jay's able to give me is two paragraphs about a flower show.'

'Sorry,' I said. 'I've got something big brewing.'

'Is it this murder in Port Logan?'

'More than that. I'll fill that double page. I promise.'

I'd have to do some pretty fast typing. Plonking myself at my desk, I said a quick hello to Jay as I turned on my computer.

'Hey Rosie,' he said. 'How do you spell—'

'Internet!' I snapped. 'It's got every word on Earth on it—and then some! And what's this I hear about not being able to spin out a story about the flower show?'

Jay mumbled. 'It's not very exciting.'

An email arrived from Todd entitled *Press Release.*

'Make it exciting!' I said. 'The show's been running for twenty years, so there's plenty of backstory in the archives. And research the plants. You've got the whole history of botany to draw on. Spin it out to five hundred words. That's an order!'

Suitably chastised, Jay started typing. I turned my attention to the press release, copied most of it into a document, and merged it with another document containing my notes.

An hour later, I fell back, exhausted. I sent the story to Harry and waited. It took an entire minute, but then his voice rang out from his office.

'Rosie!' he yelled. 'You're amazing!'

'I know!'

'Come in here!'

I trotted into his office, where he was poring over the article. 'I'm going to make a suggestion about the headline,' he said.

'You don't like, *Does a Serial Killer Haunt Port Logan?*

'Let's make it more definite: *Port Logan Serial Killer.*' He sat back. 'Rosie, you know this is the biggest story in the history of the paper?'

'Huh?'

He stared at me. 'Seriously?' he said. 'A serial killer in our tiny corner of the world? I know it's terrible news, but this will keep us busy for years.'

I hadn't thought of it that way.

'Serial killers usually have some kind of signature,' Harry continued. 'What about this guy?'

'He does,' I said, thinking of the knots left at the crime scenes. Those details weren't in my story. 'Todd asked me to keep that on the down-low for the moment.'

'Sounds juicy.'

'If I betray his confidence, I'll never get it back again.'

'Fair enough.' Harry shrugged. 'Any idea who it could be? Is it someone local? Or is a stranger using Port Logan as their hunting ground?'

I told Harry I didn't know, though I had my suspicions. The town was so small that the chances of the killer being an outsider were slim. My phone rang, and I glanced at the screen: Keith. That was a pleasant surprise. 'I better take this,' I told Harry and went outside.

'Rosie,' Keith said. 'Just wondering if you've got time for that coffee?'

'Now?'

'If you can?'

'I've always got time for coffee,' I told him.

We agreed to meet at Sandy's Diner, and a few minutes later, I was waiting for him in one of the booths. Sandy brought over my coffee as my phone rang again. This time it was Kim. I told her who I was meeting.

'Keith?' she said. 'Really? Do you think that's a good idea?'

'What do you mean?'

Kim sighed. 'I'm not so sure about him, Rosie,' she said. 'There's something about Keith that seems a bit off.'

'He's fine.' At that moment, Keith appeared. 'Got to go.' I hung up.

'Hope I wasn't interrupting anything,' Keith said, as he slid into the opposite seat. 'I know you're a busy woman.'

'There's always something happening.'

Keith ordered a black coffee.

'You drink black coffee?' I said. 'I've got a friend who does that. I don't know how you stand the taste.'

'Is it your policeman friend?'

I said *yes* and told him about Todd. 'He's a good cop,' I said. 'Much better than his predecessor.'

Keith's coffee arrived, and he took a tentative sip. 'You must feel good about the council decision.'

I shrugged. 'Keeping the boatshed will benefit the whole town. I think most people are in favour of doing something with it. A café or a snack shop would be fine. People want it transformed. Not bulldozed.'

'So this is the start of a long battle?'

'Most likely. Giuseppe will submit another development application. If he's sensible, it'll be something that retains the original building. Then it'll go back for a council vote. But, of course, the big news of the day is the Port Logan Killer.'

'I heard there'd been a murder.'

'It might be one of many.' I gave him a quick summary of the case.

Keith shook his head. 'Whoever would imagine there'd be so much action in this part of the world? Are the police close to catching him?'

'Todd Parker is a diligent investigator,' I said. 'Now that the police are on his trail, I imagine it's just a matter of time.'

Keith's phone rang. 'Sorry,' he said. 'This is business.'

Leaving me at the table, he stepped outside to speak. Without meaning to, I watched his face change as he spoke on the phone. Whatever business was being transacted, it looked pretty serious. A few minutes passed before he returned and apologised again.

'Things are a bit tense,' he said. 'It's my mother's estate. My brother's causing some dramas.'

'That's unfortunate.'

He glanced at his watch. 'I'm sorry, Rosie,' he said. 'I'd better cut this short. I've got a million things to do.'

'Me too.'

Keith paid up, and we headed outside. He was a handsome man—and he had nice manners. Both were high on my list of desirable qualities.

My thoughts turned to Todd.

What am I going to do?

20

The message from Todd came on my phone late in the afternoon.

Busy tonight?

'Hmm,' I murmured.

Jay looked up from his desk. 'What's that, Rosie?'

'Oh, just talking to myself.'

It had been a long day. As well as finishing some articles, I'd been bringing my notes up to date. Although I didn't feel like going out, I knew meeting with Todd would be a good idea. And it wasn't just because my feelings about him were more tangled than a ball of wool at the bottom of a knitter's kit. He might have more information about the killer. With any luck, some might come my way.

I headed outside and rang him.

'Todd,' I said. 'I happen to be free.'

'Then how about a bite to eat?'

'Where'd you have in mind?'

'How about Sandy's?'

'You know I eat and drink there so often that I should be a part-owner?'

'You probably should. Will I take that as a yes?'

We agreed to have an early dinner at the diner in half an hour. After saying goodbye to everyone, I decided to take a walk down to the beach. Taking the coastal path, I meandered up the hill to Cut Rock Lookout. Although the sky was clear, a light breeze had sprung up, and the waves were capped with white peaks.

I stared out at the ocean, my mind in turmoil.

There seemed to be so much going on: the Port Logan Killer, the boatshed, Nico's drug dealing, and my relationships with Todd and Keith.

I sat down on a nearby bench and looked out at the water. The sun was already low in the sky. The ocean was crashing into the huge split that cleaved the rock, sending up cascades of spray. A lot had happened in the last few days, and it had all begun with the note at my office. I pulled it from my handbag and reread it.

So strange, all these deaths in Port Logan. And now, Stewart Bard.

Whoever had sent it had wanted me to investigate the string of deaths. *All these deaths.* They had felt—or known—that Stewart Bard was the latest victim in a long line of murders.

The first was Florence Teale. Next was Jamie Farrell and then Cynthia Shepherd. Then Stewart, who had been crushed by the falling boulder, and now Karl Hoffman.

Barring Karl's death, the others could have all been tragic accidents. It was unlikely but possible. Karl's murder and the discovery of the knots had linked all the crimes.

So who was the killer?

Grace? She could have had an intense dislike of Florence, but why invite her to come and visit? Grace seemed to have money. Although she could have been interested in developing the properties around Port Logan, no mention had been made of her trying to make any purchases. The only bidding war had been between Ray and Cynthia.

So, what about Sybil? Her husband could have been her latest victim, and she killed him because of their drug business. There was a slight chance that some of the other people in town had discovered they were producing drugs.

Each of the victims could have been killed to keep their drug manufacturing secret. Again, though, that didn't explain Florence's death.

Our next suspects were Jamie's parents. Jean and Robert could be a killing couple. There were cases where husbands and wives or brothers worked together. Of course, this meant that they'd murdered their own son. That was a giant leap. My thoughts returned to the hole in their living room floor.

Although I hadn't thought twice about it before, it seemed to hold particular importance for them.

What were they hiding in that hole?

Next was Philip, who was definitely an odd character. An archaeologist, he probably had extensive knowledge of belief systems. There was a ritualistic quality to the murders: the knots left at the crime scenes. He was a possibility.

There was also Iris, who owned the shop.

By her own admission, she'd been responsible for a serious assault. As far as we knew, she was the only person in town who had a history of violence. And we only had Iris's word that she saw Raincoat leaving the burning car. She could have lied about that. I'd check with Todd over dinner to see if Iris told him about her previous conviction. Not telling him would put her in a bad light.

There were two people I could immediately dismiss: Nola and Monica Evans. The twins really would need to be vampires to cause all this mayhem, and I didn't believe in such things.

So, who was left? Ray and Robyn Pennington. No doubt about it, Ray was an unlikeable character. He'd fought with just about everyone in Port Logan, and his experience with boats gave him familiarity with knots. Finally, there was Robyn. She had an odd quality about her. A curious blankness in her personality. And she had her own secret life: the affair with Philip proved that.

There was a possibility that Ray and Robyn could be a killing couple, although I rated the chances of that as low. Their marriage seemed unstable at best. They were more like two single people sharing the same house.

I glanced at my watch. It was time to meet Todd. Heading back down the hill, I passed by the giftware store Grace had recommended. Ducking in, I bought the ceramic mouse and tucked it in my bag.

Nan will love this.

Continuing along Percy Street, I reached the diner at the same time as Todd. After some of the usual pleasantries, we headed inside. Sandy, who was wiping down the counter, gave me a broad wink as we slipped into a booth.

Good grief, I thought. *This entire town is fixated on my love life!*

'We haven't had a chance to chat about the other night,' Todd said. I stared at him blankly. 'Dinner? When I ditched you at the last moment?'

'Oh, yes,' I said. 'The other night.'

Oh, dear. Of course, I hadn't told Todd about going to the barbeque with Keith.

'I wanted to make it up to you,' he said.

'It's fine. These things happen.'

Sandy came over with some menus, and we ordered burgers, fries, and soft drinks.

'I hope you weren't too uncomfortable,' Todd continued. 'I know it's not easy dealing with ex-partners. Especially when they've moved on.'

'Well...' I began, not sure how to proceed. 'I didn't actually go alone.'

I told him about Keith. Although it was hard to read Todd's face—he obviously knew how to keep a poker face from dealing with criminals—I could still sense his disappointment.

'It's fine,' he said. 'So, are you seeing this guy again?'

The answer was probably *yes*, although saying it aloud made it sound like Keith and I were in a relationship, and we weren't.

'I don't know.'

'I see.'

Again, his face was unreadable, but those two words seemed to cover some deep hurt. I decided to change the subject and asked if he'd made any progress on the Port Logan Killer.

'Still investigating,' Todd said, seemingly relieved that we'd moved onto another topic. 'The attempt to make Karl's death look like a suicide was pretty clumsy.'

'Oh?'

'We checked his hands for gunshot residue, and there was none. Someone else shot him and put the weapon in his hand.'

I asked if Iris had spoken to him, and he said she had.

'That was a serious assault,' he said. 'But it was a long time ago. I'm glad Iris came forward because we would have found it anyway.'

'Has anyone else approached you,' I began, thinking about Sybil, 'with any startling information?'

He frowned. 'No,' he said. 'Should they?'

'Just curious.'

I averted my gaze by sipping my drink.

Todd continued. 'Do you think the killer is local?'

'I think so.'

'Your best guess?'

'Nola and Monica.'

Todd's jaw dropped. 'Those two old ladies?' he said. 'But they're—'

He saw the smile playing on my lips.

'You're terrible, Rosie.'

'I know. It comes naturally to me.'

We continued eating and had just finished our meal when Todd's phone rang. He answered it. 'What?' he snapped. 'When...how...'

He eventually hung up.

'What is it?' I asked.

'You better see for yourself.'

We hurried outside. People were standing on the foreshore, watching a fiery blaze that had erupted near the wharf. A siren cut the night: the fire brigade. It tore past us towards the burning building.

'Is that—' I started.

'The boatshed,' Todd said. 'Come on.'

We raced down. A few locals had tried to unsuccessfully arrange a bucket brigade, using water from the beach, but without success. The whole building was alight. By the time Todd and I arrived, fire was licking the rafters and was pouring through the windows.

A police car arrived, and a few cops jumped out.

Todd coordinated with them to keep back the crowds as the fire brigade hosed down the structure. My heart in my throat, I took a few photos for the paper. This was news. It was terrible news, but it was still news.

Fortunately, no one had been hurt in the blaze, although it was clear that there was one fatality.

'The boatshed's finished,' Todd said. 'And can you smell that?'

I inhaled. Beneath the stench of smoke and burning wood, there was another smell. 'Is that petrol?'

'Smells like it.'

'But who—'

'Who do you think?'

My stomach felt queasy. 'I see.' The sick feeling in my gut turned to anger. 'This is how Giuseppe Costa gets around submitting another development application. With the boatshed destroyed, he can build whatever he wants.'

'I guess that's how it works.'

'It shouldn't be.'

By now, the fire brigade was putting out the smouldering remains of the boatshed. Nothing could be salvaged. Giuseppe had gotten his way. The locals might not frequent his new business, but the tourists wouldn't know. They'd buy their fish and chips and ice creams and drinks, not knowing the price that had been paid to make that possible.

21

'What would make for a better headline?' I asked. '*Maniac Businessman Destroys Boatshed*? Or *Greedy Owner Destroys Local Heritage*?'

'They both sound totally accurate,' Ellie Applegate said. 'But I doubt Harry will approve either.'

I asked Trixie what headline she preferred, but she ignored me and laid her head on my knee.

'Harry has no imagination,' I grumbled.

We were in my office at the Gazette. It was still early in the morning, and Harry hadn't arrived yet. He was usually the first in, but he'd been caught up in a meeting with the printer.

Ellie shoved back her dreadlocks. 'This is another reason why Ralph and I live away from civilisation,' she said. 'To keep away from creeps like Giuseppe Costa.'

'It's hard to avoid them sometimes.'

I heard the front door of the office open and Harry's feet on the timber boards.

'Where's my star reporter?' he called out.

'Here I am!'

Harry leaned into my office, said hello to Ellie, and turned to me. 'Have you started the boatshed story yet?'

'I've got it half-written.'

'You need to speak to Giuseppe. Get his side of things. Also, chat to the ladies at the historical society. They'll have something to say.'

Although I wasn't looking forward to speaking to Giuseppe, I knew it had to be done.

Ellie stroked her chin thoughtfully. 'Those ladies at the historical society can be pretty feisty,' she said. 'Giuseppe had better not head down any back alleys. He might get stabbed to death with a knitting needle.'

'Hope he's got security,' Harry sighed and headed to his desk.

I rang Giuseppe's office, spoke to his secretary, and arranged a nine o'clock appointment. After hanging up, I glanced at my watch. 'That gives me just enough time to buy another coffee,' I said.

'Haven't you already had one?' Ellie asked.

'It's definitely a two coffee day,' I informed her. 'Might even be three.'

Minutes later, I was at the diner while Sandy frothed the milk for my coffee. I noticed Kim passing, and she came in to say *hi*. Although Kim looked tearful over the loss of the building, Sandy was downright angry.

'People are really riled up about Giuseppe,' Sandy told us. 'I don't suppose Todd can do anything about him?'

'Not without evidence.'

Kim sighed. 'Give me the early days of Cape Carson,' she said. 'One guy pitchforked his neighbour for stealing his milk.'

'Wow. That's pretty serious for taking a bucket of milk.'

'I know. It turned out to be the wrong neighbour too.'

'Bummer.'

Saying goodbye to them, I grabbed my coffee and headed to Giuseppe's office with Trixie. Giuseppe's secretary, Teresa, gave me a nod as I arrived. She never looked happy. Maybe working for Giuseppe made you permanently sour.

The door to his office flew open. 'Rosie!' Giuseppe said. 'What a tragic day!'

It was only through enormous effort that I didn't roll my eyes.

Yes, I thought. *Tragic you weren't in the building when it went up in flames!*

'Thanks for making some time,' I said.

'It's a pleasure, as always,' he said, waving Trixie and me into his office. 'But what a shame that we can't be meeting under better circumstances.'

I sat down. 'Yes,' I said. 'Terrible. I suppose the police have spoken to you?'

'They have,' he said. 'And I hate to point the finger, but it's pretty obvious who's responsible for the loss of the building.'

'Oh?'

'The protesters,' he said. 'Those hippies who broke in and occupied the place. The building was safe before they moved in. They take drugs. Vandalise the joint...I mean, that beautiful historic building. What can you expect?'

I stared at him. Even Trixie tilted her head in disbelief. It was amazing that Giuseppe could keep a straight face while he spoke such rubbish. I started taking notes. 'So you blame the protesters,' I said. 'You think they purposely burnt the place down? Or it was an accident?'

'It could have been either.' He leaned closer. 'Your beautiful grandmother was there. A lovely lady. We need more people like her. I know she'd never do anything destructive. It's these young people. They don't work. They sit around all day on the dole. It's a miracle the place stood for as long as it did.'

I decided to take a gamble to see how Giuseppe would react. 'At least the police might catch the person responsible,' I said. 'A few shops on that section of Percy Street have cameras facing the beach.'

Giuseppe's face fell. 'Really?' he said. 'I didn't know that.'

'Oh yes. The police will be checking those cameras. It's just a matter of time before they identify someone.'

He swallowed. 'Well,' he said. 'That's lucky.'

'Mind if I take a picture?'

Before he could answer, I whipped out my phone and snapped an image of him. It was a sight to behold. Giuseppe looked forlorn. Of course, it wasn't for the loss of the shed, but the possibility the firebug would be caught. If that happened, the trail would lead straight back to Giuseppe. I wished him a good day and walked out.

I was in reception when the fire escape door opened.

'Keith?' I said. 'What are you doing here?'

He looked as surprised as me. 'Just doing some business,' he said. 'Have you been talking to Giuseppe?'

'Yes, I've been interviewing him about the boatshed.'

'What a terrible shock! I hope they catch whoever did it and throw away the key!'

I headed downstairs.

However, instead of returning to work, I rounded the block and waited at the bottom of the fire escape. With rage burning in the pit of my stomach, I checked some information on my phone before the fire escape door finally cracked open.

'How's business?' I asked Keith as he emerged.

He swallowed. 'Fine.'

'Yeah. I'm sure. You turn up out of nowhere to deal with your mother's estate, and now our boatshed burns down. What's your mother's name again?'

Keith didn't answer.

'Maybe you've forgotten,' I said. 'Fortunately, I've got an excellent memory. Her name was Marjorie Allan, though she didn't have any sons. Only three daughters.' I was getting warmed up now. 'Is this what you do? Giuseppe beckons, and you do his dirty work for him? He wanted a spy in town, so you conveniently turned up at the Book Club. Then he needs to know what the locals are thinking, and so you turn up at the boatshed too.'

'Rosie, I—'

'That building meant something to us, Keith,' I said. 'If Keith is your real name. You probably don't know what family, friendship, and community are, but they mean something to the people of this town. Those are the things that give meaning to life. That makes life worth living!'

He tried to speak again, but I'd already marched off with Trixie at my heel. Reaching the street, I skirted past some cars and around a van. It was then that the hand gripped my arm from behind.

I swung around, ready to punch Keith in the jaw. 'Don't you—'

Except it wasn't Keith. It was Nico, and he was pushing a piece of fabric against my nose. Screaming, I flailed at him as a pungent chemical smell made me see stars. Then the stars faded to black.

I've been a fool, I thought. *I should have told Todd about Nico. Now it's too late...*

Time passed. There was nothing. Then voices drifted through the gloom.

'...shouldn't have brought her here,' the voice was saying.

Who is that? My hazy brain wondered. *It's a woman. Is it—*

I opened my eyes.

I lay on the floor of a small shed, surrounded by bags of fertiliser and garden mix. My hands were tied behind my back, and my feet were bound. My handbag sat on a shelf near the closed shed door. The only light coming in was through a single window in the side. Trixie was nowhere to be seen. There were two other people in the shed. One was Nico and the other—

Oh, dear.

'Sybil,' I said, my voice slurring.

The woman was mid-conversation with Nico. She stopped and turned to me, her face flushed. 'I'm sorry, Rosie,' she said. 'It wasn't supposed to be like this.'

'Shut up!' Nico snarled.

The woman looked close to tears.

'This is ridiculous,' I said as I tried to sit up. 'Nico, let me go, and we can talk about this.'

Nico resolutely shook his head. 'It's too late for that, Rosie,' he said. 'I always liked you. I didn't want it to come to this.'

The way he was speaking sounded awfully final.

Way too final for my liking. 'You need to think about what you're doing,' I said. 'I told a bunch of other people about your drug dealing. The sensible thing for you to do is hand yourself in.'

'If the cops knew, they would have already come knocking at my door.' Nico sounded defiant. 'All Sybil's got to do is deny everything, and we can go back to how things were.'

'And me?' I asked. 'What about me?'

His eyes settled on me. 'I'm sorry, Rosie,' Nico said. 'It's not personal. But you've brought this on yourself.'

I stared at him. It was hard to believe that this guy had been George's best man at our wedding, and he was Amanda's godfather. I'd known him for over twenty years. The more I looked, though, I realised that guy was long gone.

Drug addiction had transformed him.

Taken him down a dead-end road.

'How do you work that out?' I asked.

'You could never leave things alone. You never stop. You keep digging and digging. On and on. If you'd stuck to writing stories about boatsheds and council meetings, you'd...well...' He stopped. 'Well, now look where you are.'

I could see where I was. My ex-brother-in-law was getting ready to kill me.

'There's something I need to know,' I said.

'What?'

'How much does George know?'

Nico hesitated. 'George knows I've been using,' he said. 'But he and Sadie don't know about the dealing. They've been trying to get me to stop.'

'I see.'

Reaching into his jacket, Nico pulled out a knife. Sybil let out a small cry as she shrank back. My eyes narrowed on the blade.

'We went to the Smuggler's Inn last night,' I said. 'We saw you dealing. This is all over, Nico. The only person who doesn't know that is you. Now untie me, and we'll go to the police. I promise I'll do whatever I can to help you.'

'No,' Nico said. 'It's moved past that.'

Nico's face was expressionless, without the slightest shred of humanity. It was like staring into a black hole. Maybe that's how it was with killers. They disassociated themselves from their deeds. Allowed evil, inner logic to justify their actions. To justify murder. To justify anything.

As he took a step towards me, the shed door rattled open, and a man in a balaclava appeared. Sybil screamed. Nico turned, yelled, and raised the knife but was no match for the newcomer. The man leaped at him, slammed a fist into his chin, and Nico's eyes rolled up into his head. He toppled unconscious to the ground.

The man turned to Sybil. 'Out!' he snapped.

Semi-hysterical, Sybil staggered from the shed as the new-comer snatched up the knife and cut through my bindings. I stood up shakily. The man fetched my handbag and helped me outside. I blinked at the bright sunlight. Sybil was sitting on a pile of garden sleepers, weeping uncontrollably.

I'm alive, I thought with a kind of wonder. *I'm alive.*

A frenzied barking started, and I saw Trixie. She was tied to a nearby stake in the ground, and I untied her before turning back to the masked man. Concern filled his green eyes. 'Are you all right?' he murmured.

'I'm okay,' I said, although now my whole body was shaking. 'We need to get out of here.'

The man crossed to the shed. He closed and padlocked the door. Taking a phone from his pocket, he made a call using a gutteral, disguised voice.

'A woman's been assaulted at the Crawley Street Garden Centre,' he said. 'She needs medical attention. The man who assaulted her is locked in a shed.'

The voice at the other end started asking questions, but the man ended the call.

'I'd better go,' he said. 'The police will be here shortly.' He gave my arm a quick squeeze. 'It's been nice knowing you, Rosie Ryan. Hope we meet up again sometime.'

My rescuer hurried away, disappearing onto the street and

out of sight. A wailing siren cut through the afternoon air as a desperate pounding and yelling came from the shed.

'Oh,' I muttered. 'Be quiet.'

22

'You're sure you can't identify this man?' Todd asked.

I shook my head. 'He was wearing a balaclava,' I said. 'He could walk past me on the street, and I wouldn't know him.' I turned to the doctor. 'When can I go? I'm feeling absolutely fine.'

'Give us a few more minutes.' The doctor's name was Sam Tyler. He was a nice young man with soft brown eyes and a newcomer to Cape Carson Hospital. 'Just to make certain there's no aftereffects from the chloroform.'

I agreed, although I intended on hightailing it out of there as soon as possible. Barring a few scratches and a slightly woozy head, I felt okay. After Todd and another constable had turned up, they'd taken both Nico and Sybil away. Although Nico wasn't saying much, Sybil was singing like a bird. Her house had been searched by the police, and the Federal authorities were raiding another place in Melbourne.

I reached down and scratched Trixie's head. Nico had left

her abandoned on the street. It was my masked hero who had brought her to the garden centre.

Kim appeared in the doorway. 'Rosie!'

'Kim!'

Ignoring the doctor's protests, I climbed out of bed, and we had a huge hug. Todd gently informed Kim that he was interviewing me, but she would have none of it.

'Get in line,' she said. 'It's not everyday my best friend gets almost killed by her ex-brother-in-law.'

'Hopefully, it'll be the last time.'

'Now,' Kim said, 'tell me what happened.'

I went through my story again, going into the same level of detail as I had with Todd. Kim knew me well enough to sense that I was holding something back.

'So a mysterious masked man came to your rescue?' she said. 'That's amazing.'

'Incredible,' I agreed.

I asked Doctor Tyler if I could go, and he reluctantly agreed. He could see that trying to keep me at the hospital was a waste of time. The doctor wished me well and left as I scooped up my handbag.

'Come on,' I said to Kim and Todd. 'Let's head down to Sandy's. I'm sure only coffee can counteract the effects of the chloroform.'

'I'm surprised the doctor didn't prescribe a jumbo double

shot caramel latte,' Todd said.

'I know. Most remiss of him. And he seemed so competent.'

Minutes later, the three of us were nestled into a booth at Sandy's and drinking our caffeine of choice.

'So when were you going to tell me about this drug lab?' Todd asked. 'You know that not informing the police about Sybil made you an accessory after the fact? You can be charged for concealing a crime?'

He sounded very Mister Policeman and not like my friend at all. In fact, he sounded downright annoyed. I suppose I couldn't blame him. He was right, and I was wrong.

'I'm sorry,' I said, and I meant it. I explained that I'd wanted Sybil to come forth of her own accord. 'Sadly, she didn't do that.'

Todd frowned. 'All right,' he said. 'Don't do it again.'

'I promise I'll never break the law again.'

The big policeman stroked his chin. 'Of course,' he said. 'We now have another issue: The Masked Avenger who came to your aid.' He paused. 'Or your secret admirer.'

My gaze met his. 'Just someone who was there at the right time.' I needed to divert this conversation before it got too personal. 'Have you had any success finding who burned down the boatshed?'

'Not yet. We're still checking footage from the Percy Street businesses.'

Nodding, I decided to check my phone for images I'd taken on the night. I may have looked calm on the surface, but my emotions were churning underneath. Keith had to be arrested for what he'd done. Giuseppe had paid him to infiltrate our group and burn down our local landmark, all in the name of profit.

And yet, Keith had come to my rescue when Nico kidnapped me. Although his face had been covered, there was no mistaking those green eyes looking at me from beyond the mask. Thinking about Keith Yaeger—if that was his real name—made my mind whirl.

Keith was a bad guy. He'd broken the law. I had to do whatever I could to bring him to justice—even if he had saved my life.

Todd's eyes were still on me. To avoid his gaze, I skimmed through the pictures on my phone. I'd taken a lot over the last week, most of which I'd have to delete.

Gosh, I thought. *Some of these are awful.*

The worst were the pictures I'd dutifully taken of Ray's paintings. As an artist, he was a better Elvis impersonater. I scrolled through the images.

'Wait a minute,' I said.

'What is it?' Kim asked.

I looked up at her and Todd, my heart pounding. 'Ray's pictures,' I said, showing them my phone. 'Notice anything?'

Todd skimmed through them. 'There's a picture of a boat in the bay,' he said. 'Another of the headland. A painting of Karl's home. And one from the top of the hill...' His eyes angled up to mine. 'These are the crime scenes.'

I turned to Kim. 'You remember how I was getting that weird feeling of déjà vu? *This is why!* Those are all locations that Ray has painted. He paints a picture of the place before he murders someone. He's the killer!'

Kim slowly nodded. 'And they're not even good paintings!'

'Okay, ladies,' Todd said. 'I understand your enthusiasm. There *seems* to be a correlation between Ray's paintings and the crime scenes, but—'

'Let me guess,' I said. 'You need evidence. Real physical evidence.'

'That's kind of how it works.'

I felt like yelling at Todd. It couldn't be a coincidence that Ray had painted at each of the crime scenes.

Still, yelling wouldn't get us anywhere. You couldn't arrest someone because of a painting.

'All right,' I said.

He frowned. 'Really? You're fine with that?'

'I'll just have to keep digging until I find something.'

Todd wasn't used to me being so accommodating. 'And here I was thinking you were going to yell and scream,' he said. 'Maybe even punch me in the nose.'

'I only do that to people who are *extra* special.' I nodded to Kim. 'I've punched Kim in the nose six times.'

'Seven,' Kim said, straight-faced. 'But who's counting?'

Todd regarded us suspiciously as he finished his coffee. 'All right,' he said. 'I'd better get moving. Like I said before, let me know if you come across any real evidence. While the paintings are a good start, we need more. And for goodness sake, Rosie—be careful!'

I promised I would. Todd left and I turned to Kim with renewed determination. 'Guess what we're going to do?'

'Probably not spending the night watching old films?'

'Not even close. We're heading back to Port Logan to find evidence that proves Ray is the killer.'

Kim, Trixie, and I were soon zooming down Millicent Drive in my jeep. It was late in the day now, and clouds were coming in from the west. Lightning flashed on the horizon.

'The radio said a storm is coming,' Kim observed.

'Making it the perfect night to track down a killer.'

Kim sighed. 'And this is coming from the woman who doesn't like horror films.'

We were soon pulling into Nola and Monica's driveway. Just as I stopped the car, my phone rang: Amanda.

'I'd better take this,' I told Kim.

'I'll help the old girls with dinner.'

She disappeared inside with Trixie as I took the call.

'Darling daughter,' I said with trepidation.

'Don't give me any darling daughter rubbish! What's this I hear about Uncle Nico getting arrested? And him trying to kill you?'

I told her what had happened, leaving out the identity of my saviour. It was only at the end that Amanda burst into tears.

'Oh, mum,' she sobbed. 'That's awful. I used to ride on Nico's shoulders when I was little! We played hide and seek at our old house!'

'I know, honey.'

In the midst of my excitement of investigating Ray, I'd forgotten how Nico's arrest would affect everyone. George would be shattered. My mum and dad, who lived in Melbourne, would be shocked. Nan would be disappointed.

Then there were George's parents. They were Amanda's grandparents, her *papa* and *yaya*, as she called them. They were divorced but stayed in contact with George and Nico. What would they make of this?

Amanda sniffed away her tears. 'Are you sure he was going to kill you?' she asked. 'I mean, *really* kill you?'

I thought about him with the knife. 'It certainly looked that way,' I said.

'But Nico was never like that.'

'It's the drugs.' The words seemed to hang in the air. 'He wasn't thinking straight. I don't think he's been straight for a long time.'

The more I spoke about it, the more upset I felt. Although Nico and I had never been best friends, we'd been friendly. He'd helped George and me a dozen times over in those early years of our marriage.

'I'll put in a good word for him,' I said. 'But I can't lie. The guy was violent. He assaulted me and threatened Sybil. Nico has a serious drug addiction, and he'll go to jail for what he's done. Maybe he'll use that time to straighten himself out.'

'Some people come out of jail worse than when they went in.'

'Then it's up to Nico to change himself.' I hesitated. 'This is a turning point, and what direction he takes is up to him.'

Amanda said she had better see her dad. I hung up and went into Nola and Monica's place. A lovely aromatic flavour filled the air.

'My goodness,' I said. 'What's cooking?'

'Lamb casserole,' Nola said, appearing briefly from the kitchen. 'One of my specialties.'

'I'm sure.'

The woman returned to the kitchen, and Kim sidled up to me. 'There was a tiny mishap,' she told me quietly. 'The ladies had run out of lamb.'

'Okay,' I said slowly. 'So...'

'They've used chicken instead.'

Right, I thought. *We're having lamb casserole...made with chicken.*

Kim and I set the table, and within the hour, we were sitting around enjoying the hearty casserole. The ladies had seen the police pouring in and out of Sybil's home. They asked me about what had happened with Sybil, so I told them about her involvement in the drug trade. Nola asked me if we'd made any headway on the Port Logan monster.

'Uh,' I said. 'Not really. I'm not sure there is one.'

'Give it time,' Monica said. 'It'll reveal itself to you when it's ready.'

'Okay.'

'What about Karl?' Nola asked. 'Do you know who killed him?'

'Not yet,' Kim said. 'The police are looking at everyone.'

'Everyone?' Monica said, her eyes sparkling. 'Goodness. That means we're suspects!'

'Suspects!' Nola repeated, relishing the idea. 'Suspects in a murder investigation. Imagine that. At our age!'

'Which means they're examining everyone's motives.' She turned to her sister. 'Karl could be downright rude sometimes. More than once he barged past us on the path.'

'Is that enough to kill someone over?'

Monica grinned. 'I don't know,' she said. 'Is it?'

The two old ladies burst out laughing.

'Hope you've got alibis,' I said.

'Only each other!' Nola said.

'We could get grilled at the police station,' Monica said. 'But they won't break me. Any questions, I'll just say *No comment.*'

'Me too,' Nola agreed, glancing down at our plates. 'Have you had enough to eat?'

'No comment,' Kim said, and everyone laughed.

If they had been physically capable of killing anyone, I would have added them to our suspect list. Fortunately, their fragile states excluded them from being real suspects.

Unless they're actually…vampires.

But that was a silly idea.

Wasn't it?

We thanked them for their hospitality and insisted on washing the dishes. By now, night had fallen, and I was feeling tired. As much as I would have loved to have gotten to bed early, I was determined to keep moving forward on our investigation.

Returning to our little room, I changed into dark clothing and suggested that Kim do the same.

'O-kay,' she said slowly. 'What do you have in mind?'

'I want to check out Ray's place from the dunes,' I said. 'It should give us a clear view.'

'And then?'

I gave her an innocent look. 'We'll see.'

'Rosie,' Kim said, frowning. 'Are you sure about this? You're not about to do anything stupid, are you?'

'As if I'd do that.'

'I'm serious. You've already had someone try to kill you once today.'

'I know,' I said, a trifle annoyed. 'I was there.'

'If Ray's the Port Logan Killer, then he won't hesitate to bump you off.'

'I won't do anything foolish. I promise.'

'I can always tell when you're fibbing,' she said. 'And you're fibbing now.'

'Don't be silly. Now come on!'

Leaving Trixie behind, we skirted around the bay to Iris Kelly's shop. The town was in darkness now, with the moon flickering behind scudding clouds, and rain was in the air.

Distant lightning flashed across the ocean. The storm was getting closer.

'Look,' I hissed as we took refuge in the shadows. 'Their car's not in the driveway.'

'They must be out for the night,' Kim said.

Ray was probably busy being Elvis, while Robyn may have been spending the evening with Philip. Kim and I continued west up Oxley street and came up the dunes behind the houses. The only light was the television in Grace's home. Ray and Robyn's place lay in darkness.

We took refuge behind the shattered fence line. I pointed to the back door. 'You remember Ray said no one ever locks their doors around here,' I said. 'I bet their back door is unlocked.'

'It probably is.'

I'd been thinking about this since making the connection between the crime scenes and the paintings. 'Ray's probably got a hidey-hole where he keeps trophies from his crimes. If we can find that, then this case is solved.'

Kim glared at me in the darkness. 'Rosie,' she said. 'You're talking about breaking into someone's home. What if you get caught?'

'I won't get caught.'

'But you might.' Kim gripped my arm. 'And didn't you promise Todd only a few hours ago that you wouldn't break the law? You *promised*.'

She was right. I had promised, and I didn't feel good about breaking that promise, but a serial killer was on the loose. The evidence to bring him to justice was probably only a few feet away. Who knew what Ray might do with that evidence? If he hadn't already disposed of it, then it was only a matter of time.

'I know,' I said grudgingly. 'But sometimes promises have to be broken.'

'Rosie, this isn't some abandoned house; it's someone's home. And you don't have any actual evidence that Ray's the killer.'

Lightning flashed in the distance and I glimpsed concern in

Kim's face.

'Okay,' I said. 'What about the paintings?'

'The paintings aren't real evidence. No court would count them as meaning anything. It could just be a coincidence that he's painted those places.'

'Now you're being ridiculous!'

Kim folded her arms. '*I'm* being ridiculous?' she said. 'What if Ray is the killer? A real honest-to-goodness serial killer. It means he's already killed five people. What if he finds you searching his home? He won't hesitate to kill you!'

'That's why I need you to keep a lookout.'

'I'm not keeping a lookout,' Kim said stubbornly. 'Searching a serial killer's home for evidence is insane!'

'Ah-ha! So even you think he's a serial killer!'

'I don't know what he is, but it's wrong to break into a person's house. What if he's innocent? What if it were your home? Doesn't everyone deserve their privacy?'

Now I was stubborn. 'Yes, I do, but I'm not a murderous monster who's killed five people! Are you going to be my lookout or not?'

'No, I'm not! I'm going back to Nola and Monica's place. And I'm eating the rest of the lamb casserole. Or chicken casserole. Whatever it is!'

'Okay! Go back! Eat the casserole! I don't care!'

'Fine!'

'Fine!'

Kim marched off through the sand and out of sight. Seeing her disappear from view made me want to burst into tears. Kim and I had argued over the years, but I'd never seen her so angry.

Is this my fault? I wondered. *Am I doing the wrong thing?*

Kim was right. In my heart, I knew it, but the images of Ray's paintings kept going through my head. It was too much of a coincidence that he had painted every crime scene. Even Todd had admitted it looked bad. All we needed was evidence that would link him to the murders.

I ducked between some broken palings and across the sandy yard to the back door. Activating the torch on my phone, I shone it at the back screen door and listened hard. No sound came from inside. All I could hear was a distant rumble of thunder. I carefully turned the back door handle.

Yes!

It was unlocked! I stepped through to the hallway and shone my torch about. Here was the laundry. Nothing exciting to be found. I moved down the hall to what appeared to be a guest bedroom. The next room was a gym, complete with weight benches and a treadmill. My light reflected harshly off the mirrors lining the back wall.

Ray likes looking at himself, I thought. *No surprise there.*

Next, I came across the master bedroom. Like the rest of

the house, it seemed strangely sterile. I paused at the doorway. It was unlikely that Ray would leave victim trophies lying around where Robyn could find them. I was also beginning to feel guilty about searching the house. It was one thing to talk about and an entirely different thing to do. I didn't relish going through Ray and Robyn's personal belongings.

Deciding to leave their bedroom till last, I went around the rest of the house. The living room revealed nothing, and I only briefly scrutinised the kitchen. That wasn't Ray's domain. I bet he didn't even know how to boil a pot of water.

I paused, undecided. Ray didn't own a back shed, but he did own a garage, and that was likely his domain. A set of stairs led under the house. The door at the bottom opened up onto a garage that smelt of linseed oil and paint.

This is where he keeps his art supplies.

Benches ran along opposite sides of the room. One was a painting bench. Judging by the vast quantity of tubes of paint and brushes, what Ray lacked in talent, he made up for in equipment. Hanging from nails along the wall were almost two dozen brushes ranging from fan-shaped brushes to ones for fine detail. A line of blank canvases sat ready for use.

Taking up pride of place on the painting bench was his current work.

Good grief.

I felt sick.

The half-completed painting was Nola and Monica's place. *They're his next victims!* I quickly began searching the opposite bench. The surface was bare, but the shelves were packed with a plethora of different things: piles of magazines, an old car battery, bags of clothing, boxes of screws, an ancient fishing box, and assorted pieces of wood that looked to be part of some abandoned joinery project.

There's nothing here.

I swung my torch about to see an anorak-clad figure in the doorway.

Biting off a scream, I refocused and saw that what appeared to be a figure was just an anorak hanging on the back of the door. I swallowed, and shock was quickly replaced by elation. *The anorak was green!* Now I rechecked the shelves with new enthusiasm, going through the items again, one at a time. Then I searched under the bench again. This time I opened the toolbox and checked inside. There was nothing other than screwdrivers and a few spanners.

I was ready to head back upstairs when I peered up at the top shelf. At first glance, it was empty and too high for most people to reach. Standing on my toes, I felt carefully along the back.

Nothing. Then—

What's that?

The tips of my fingers brushed against something, and I

reached further, angling the object around so I could grab it properly. The light on my phone danced as I dragged it down: a woman's handbag.

What's this doing up here?

Unclipping the top, I peered inside to see a purse, makeup, a packet of tissues, and other items.

What on Earth...

I opened the purse. There was no driver's licence, but there was a Medicare and pensioner's card. I read the name:

Florence Teale.

I gasped. *My goodness!* This handbag belonged to Grace's friend, who had been run over. I felt further along the top shelf. My fingers raked another object and I dragged down a mobile phone. Could this have belonged to Florence? No. The picture on the back was a heavy metal rock band.

Jamie's parents said his mobile phone was never recovered. This was why. Ray took it to keep as a trophy after killing him. Reaching up, I found other objects: a shattered, bloody watch and a woman's hairbrush. The watch must have belonged to Stewart and the hairbrush to Cynthia. There didn't seem to be anything from Karl's death. Maybe Ray was yet to add that latest trophy to his collection.

I felt all the way along the far end of the shelf. My fingers stroked another item. Even before pulling it down, I knew what it was.

Yes, I was right: a length of rope with the distinctive red strand. This was the evidence I needed!

There was the roar of an engine and then headlights flashed through the garage window. A vehicle braked. I jammed the rope and other objects into the handbag and went racing up the stairs just as the garage door started to rise. I flew through the back door, easing it shut behind me, and sprinted across the yard. Ducking under the fence, my head smashed into a loose paling. *Ouch!* Seeing stars, I staggered into the dunes.

The night closed in around me. My head hurt, but I wasn't concerned. *Ray Pennington is a serial killer.* The thought kept going around my mind. *Ray Pennington is a serial killer.* The evidence I'd found would put him away for life.

A figure emerged from the gloom to my left.

'Rosie?'

My heart almost stopped, but then I recognised the voice: Grace.

'Grace,' I gushed. 'My goodness. Sorry, I thought you were someone else.'

She activated the light on her phone. 'Rosie,' she said, peering at the object under my arm. 'What is that?'

'It's Florence's handbag,' I said, giddy with excitement.

'Where did you get it?'

'Ray Pennington's place,' I said, unable to contain myself. 'He's a killer...I mean...the killer. He's killed a lot of people, including Florence.' I was babbling. 'I was in his place and found it.'

'My goodness. But look at your head. You're bleeding.'

I touched my forehead and saw blood on my fingers. 'I ran into a fence,' I explained.

'Come to my place. I'll get you a bandaid, and a glass of port to relax.'

'I need to ring the police.'

'Not before we bandage your head.'

She was right. Blood was trickling down my face. I applied pressure to the wound as the rain started to come down. I followed Grace into her home. It was a welcome reprieve after the craziness of wandering about Ray and Robyn's place in the dark. Grace led me into her study, where a large timber desk and chesterfield captain's chair dominated the room. A laptop sat on the desk. Bookshelves lined the walls. Surrounding a small oak coffee table was an old cracked red leather lounge.

Grace splashed some port into a glass. 'Sit down, and I'll find my first aid kit.' She crossed the room, pausing at the door. 'You know, the night Florence was killed, I saw Ray returning to his home late. I always thought there was something strange about that.'

'Sometimes it takes us a while to put two and two together,' I said.

She disappeared into the other room as I plonked into one of her comfy lounge chairs. My head had almost stopped bleeding. It was just a scratch. Sitting was impossible, especially after everything I'd been through, so I got up and started pacing.

I've tracked down a serial killer.

The idea seemed preposterous.

Little old Rosie Ryan has single-handedly cracked the case!

The police would arrive, and Ray would be dragged off to jail. Harry had been right when he said this was the biggest case the area had ever seen.

My thoughts returned to Kim. I felt terrible about our fight. She'd be more understanding once she knew that I'd discovered the identity of the Port Logan killer. Nursing the glass of port, I strode over to Grace's bookshelf and then her desk. My eyes took in the various objects: the laptop, pen container, sheets of writing paper.

I've seen that paper recently, I thought. *Was it at a shop in Cape Carson or—*

I stared at the paper. It was light blue with a double-orange line running across the top. The reason it was familiar was because the same paper had been used for the note I'd received at the office.

So strange, all these deaths in Port Logan. And now, Stewart Bard.

It was too much of a coincidence that Grace owned the same paper; it was too uncommon. Grace sent me the note.

I tried to process this.

Grace sent me the note.

There was no sign of the typewriter, but something like that could be hidden away.

All right. Grace sent me the note.

I tried to make sense of this, but I had an eerie sensation as if I were on a merry-go-round and the rest of the world was whirling around me. Maybe I'd hit my head harder than I thought. Rain pounded the window as thunder groaned across the sky.

Why didn't Grace ring me with her suspicions?

The thought was like a sour taste in my mouth. *Why all the cloak and dagger?* Grace could have contacted me at the newspaper about the string of deaths. She didn't need to send me an unsigned note. Maybe she wanted to remain anonymous. Some people did. If she'd rung me, I would have heard her out, but I suppose the note was more engaging. More likely to pique my curiosity. A hook into a mystery.

I swallowed. And she'd just told me that she suspected Ray from the beginning. *I saw Ray returning to his home late. I always thought there was something strange about that.* Why did Grace not tell me that before? Why share it with me now?

It was almost as if Grace had wanted me to track down Ray myself.

My stomach churned uneasily.

How much more believable it is to discover the truth yourself. Grace could have told me her suspicions, and I might have investigated. Might. An unsigned note, and the mystery that ensued, was far more likely to drag me in. Because of that note, I interviewed all the locals. Put in the footwork. Unravelled the mystery. Made the connection to Ray's paintings. Broke into his home. Solved the case.

But what if I were wrong?

What if Grace were the killer?

That makes no sense. If she were a serial killer, the last thing she'd do would be to bring attention to herself. She never would have written the note.

I tried to think clearly.

The first person to die was Florence Teale. Her old neighbour had travelled across the country to visit her. Why would Grace murder an old friend she hadn't seen for years? The second to die was Jamie Farrell. Then Cynthia Shephard. Stewart Bard. And now, Karl Hoffman.

I shook my head. *This is ridiculous. Ray is the killer.* He painted each of the crime scenes and left a tied knot as his calling card. It was like something out of a movie. I clenched my jaw. It *was* like a movie. Almost *too much* like a movie. It was the stuff of which great stories are made.

The knot linked each of the crimes, but each victim died differently. Was anything else different?

I thought for a long moment. The first murder occurred a long time before the other deaths. There was a gap of more than a year. *Why the gap?* Sometimes killers hesitated before killing again. Then the urge to kill becomes so irresistible that they kill again and again until they're caught.

But why kill Florence? Why kill someone you hadn't seen for years? Grace was supposed to be picking up Florence from the top of the hill, but they got the dates mixed up. That's what Grace had said. Florence had flown from Western Australia to Melbourne and caught the bus from there. That was a long, exhausting bus ride. Why had Grace allowed an old friend to travel all that distance by bus? Why not drive to Melbourne and collect her from there? Then they could have chatted all the way back to Port Logan.

Unless she had to kill Florence.

But why kill a defenceless old lady?

I thought back to the pictures on the wall in Grace's library. They were of Grace and her sister. What was her name? That's right. Karen. She'd died in that horrible boating accident when she caught that fish and fell into the water. And there was the picture of Grace on her wedding day. Another of Karen teaching at school.

The door behind me opened, and Grace appeared with a first aid kit. 'Sorry about that,' she said. 'Good thing it wasn't a major emergency. This thing took ages to find. I rang the police too. They should be here soon.'

My stomach did a slow turn. 'It must be wonderful to be ambidextrous,' I said.

'Pardon?'

'Ambidextrous. You know. Being able to use both left and right hands equally well.'

Grace stared at me. Then, slowly, her mouth turned down, and her eyes hardened into two tiny black pebbles.

'Of course,' I continued. 'You're not ambidextrous. You're left-handed.' I pushed on. 'And you didn't ring the police.'

'What do you mean? I rang them—'

'And you knew that was Florence's handbag.'

'I...I guessed...'

'It wasn't a guess. You stared directly at the bag and asked about it. What a strange thing to notice. Fair enough, I was wandering about in the dark and took you by surprise. But why mention the bag? Of course, we both know why you mentioned it. You *recognised* it because you planted it in Ray's home. You knew it would be found one day, but you didn't expect it to be me. You thought it would be the police.'

'Rosie.' Grace's cheeks had turned bright red. 'How hard did you hit your head? You're suggesting I killed Florence? Why would I murder one of my oldest friends? And all those other people?'

'You're right. That's the most baffling piece of the puzzle. A person could be a serial killer and murder at random. After all, a serial killer operates according to their own twisted logic. But a sane person could also have their own reason or, if you like, reasons. Two reasons.

'You and your sister look very similar, especially in pictures. You're almost identical. Most people wouldn't be able to tell you apart. Of course, someone who had known both of you all your lives would know. They might not be able to tell over the phone, but in person, they'd know. It must have been irritating when Florence started ringing you to talk over old times. The old lady from Coopertell who'd known you so well.

'You must have tried talking her out of visiting, but those old ladies can be quite persistent. They won't take no for an answer. You knew the deception you'd pulled on everyone wouldn't work with Florence. Not in person. No, she'd know in seconds that you were a fraud.'

Grace's face had turned from crimson to white. She looked like a ghastly clown with two tiny red blotches showing on her pale cheeks. 'All right,' she snarled. 'Say it!'

'You're not Grace Vickery,' I said. 'You're Karen Vickery.'

The woman said nothing. She glared at me with hatred in her eyes. If a look were capable of killing, then she would have struck me dead. Everything she had done, everything she had planned, everything she had set in motion had been turned upside down.

'You're left-handed,' I continued. 'You were the teacher in the photo writing on the blackboard with your left hand. Downstairs, Grace—the real Grace—is signing the marriage register with her right hand. When you gave me the address where I could buy the ceramic mouse, you wrote with your left hand. I didn't notice at the time. It was only when I saw the writing paper up here that it all came together.

'I'm not sure if you murdered Grace's husband. Tractor accidents happen.' I swallowed. 'But you murdered Grace. It's too perfect a crime to have been formulated on the spur of the moment. You both looked similar. At one time, your hair was long, and Grace's was short, but it's easy for someone to change their hair.

'You knew Grace's PIN numbers for her accounts, and you could approximate her signature. Coopertell was thousands of miles away. You were strangers in a strange land. To become Grace, all you had to do was tell people you were her. You went out on that boat as Karen, but you returned to shore as Grace.

'Of course, you had to be careful. A quiet life was a safe life. Everything was fine until Florence contacted you and insisted on visiting. You couldn't talk her out of it, so she had to die.' I stopped. 'What didn't make sense was all the other killings. Why kill all those other people? True, it could have been to hide your first murder. To muddy the waters, but that's—no pun intended—overkill.

'It was Ray,' I said. 'You told us you had a relationship with Karl, but your relationship was really with Ray. We were told he has affairs all over the place. You were another one of his flings. To him, just another desperate woman. He dumped you without hesitation and moved on. But you didn't move on. No, as the old expression goes, *Hell hath no fury like a woman scorned*. You could have killed Ray, but that wasn't enough. You sent me the note to bring attention to him. You had to *hurt* him. Destroy him. Ruin his name, his reputation, his life—'

'Shut up!' Karen Vickery screamed. 'Shut up!'

Now she was on her feet, and I saw the long-bladed kitchen knife in her hand. She must have kept it hidden as she returned to the room.

Karen pointed the weapon at me. 'You are so smart,' she said. 'Yes, Ray had to pay for what he did. He laughed at me when he broke it off. Laughed at me and called me a silly woman! Said I was boring. I threatened to tell his wife, but that made no difference. He said Robyn knew all about his affairs and turned a blind eye because she had her own affairs.

'It was nothing to him, but it was something to me. Oh yes, it was something! I could have killed him. It's easy after the first time. You're right about Grace. She *always* had boyfriends. *Always* went on dates. Men *always* chased her. All I ever had were the leftovers.

'Grace marrying Adam was the last straw. I loved Adam and wanted him for myself. But Grace couldn't allow that. Oh no! Grace had to have him. She married Adam, and I was left out in the cold—again!

'That's why I arranged that little accident for Adam. That day, I went to the farm, pretending to drop off something for him. He was in one of the paddocks after rain. When he climbed down into a ditch to rescue one of his dogs, I drove the tractor over the edge. It only took a moment, and I felt so good. I finally had retribution for being the lesser sister!

'I pretended to grieve, but that was easy for me. I've always been a good actress. People have trusted me when I've told them things. After Adam died, I needed Grace to trust me more than ever. I convinced her that a trip around Australia would get her mind off things. Getting her onto that boat in the lake was the hardest thing. Being a non-swimmer, she didn't want to go. But she trusted me. One good push was all it took, and she was gone.'

I stared at Karen in horror. It was as if the mask had finally dropped from her face. She literally looked and sounded like a different person.

'And you're right about Ray,' she continued. 'Killing him was too easy. He had to suffer! And what better way to do that? The great man of Port Logan, reduced to nothing! The man with family, heritage, and wealth languishing in a filthy cell for life!

'The idea came to me when I saw him painting at the top of the hill. It was the place where I killed Florence. Ray was always painting around Port Logan. Why not kill people at those locations? Then Ray would become the logical suspect. I placed the handbag and other items in his garage, where I knew he'd never find them. The same with the rope. That was his rope. I just took some of it and put the rest where he couldn't reach it. All that knotted rope has his DNA on it. That evidence would put him away forever.'

'But no one followed the trail,' I said.

'People are such *fools*!' Karen spat. 'I had to draw attention to him.'

'So you sent me the letter.'

'Once you were here, and Karl was dead, I knew it would only be a matter of time before the police made the connection.' She wearily shook her head. 'The second I mentioned the handbag, I knew I'd made a mistake. How silly of me. Well, it's too late now, and it's actually good to talk about it. They say confession's good for the soul.'

'Karen,' I said. 'I hope you're not going to do anything silly with that knife.'

I'd already been threatened once with a knife in the last twenty-four hours and that was one time too often as far as I was concerned.

'Not silly,' Karen Vickery said, taking a deep breath. 'I've come this far. When you've killed as many times as I have, one more death doesn't make a difference.'

I glanced towards the door. I'd never make it through the house. She'd catch me on the stairs. My only chance was to escape through the rear and into the dunes. It was dark out there and raining. Out there I'd have a chance of surviving.

'I don't hate you, Rosie,' Karen said. 'If it's any consolation.'

'It's not,' I said. 'And, frankly, I can't stand you.'

I snatched up the lightweight coffee table, hurled it at her, and dove for the door. The table crashed into her. Screaming, she gave chase as I raced through her house and out the back door. I charged through the gloomy yard, the wind and rain tearing at my face, and out to the sandy dunes beyond.

'Help!' I screamed. 'Help!'

My voice was swept away by the wind.

The fence line lay in deep shadow, so I aimed for the dunes ahead. Karen would be on me in a second if I tried to angle along the side of the fences. She knew this territory, and I didn't. I had to put as much distance between us as possible. Charging across the dunes, I aimed for the water's edge. The sand was firmer there and would allow me to run faster.

Oof!

My foot caught on a patch of spinifex, and I went flying. I hit the sand, rolled, and was back on my feet in seconds. In that brief moment, I'd spotted Karen close behind, knife in hand, a crazed expression on her face.

I reached the shoreline. The rain had stopped, but a head-wind pushed against me as I ran. Karen was about ten metres behind, moving like a gazelle.

By comparison, I was a lumbering wombat. It was only a matter of time before she reached me.

The only way to survive this was to veer towards the dunes and lose myself in the darkness. That wasn't easy here, though, as the beach angled up sharply. I'd have to try. To continue like this was certain death.

My thoughts returned to Kim.

Kim, I thought. *You were right! Why didn't I listen to you!*

The moon momentarily took refuge behind a cloud and the whole section of coast darkened. I charged for the sand dunes. It took a moment for Karen to react. Then I heard her change direction.

The slog up the dunes became harder. The moon escaped from its cloudy veil, and I saw Karen catching up, her shadow dancing on the sand behind her. Seven metres. Five metres. My head was pounding, and my lungs were ready to explode.

With a final enormous effort, I came up over the crest of the sand—and looked on with horror at what lay ahead: a thick wall of coastal correa, a metre high bush that blocked the dunes. I couldn't go forward. I had to angle back to the shore.

Weaving wildly, I darted back down the sand. There was another sound now: not the wind or the rain or the surf. The sound of breathing. Karen's breathing. She was only a few feet behind.

I'll try to escape into the water.

But even as I had this thought, I knew it was hopeless. No sooner would I hit the water than I would slow down. And then Karen would throw herself on me like a cheetah taking down a zebra. I had to make my stand. It was now or never.

As I reached the waterline, I turned to face the crazed killer. I saw her, the knife, the shadow behind her, and then—

'Aaaarrgggh!'

The shadow leaped onto Karen's back, slamming her face forward into the sand.

That's no shadow! I realised. *It's—*

'Kim!' I screamed.

I dived onto the killer as Kim struggled with the woman. At the same instant, the distant blue and red flashing lights of a police car cut across the remote dunes as a siren split the night. The killer snarled and fought and screamed, but we wrestled the knife away. With our combined weight on her, she realised she would never escape. Her body went limp, and she let out a cry of rage that subsided to helpless weeping. She knew it was done. All the murders and the lies would finally be revealed.

Kim looked into my face. 'Rosie,' she said. 'You're the most annoying person I've ever known.'

'Kim. You were right, and I was wrong.'

'I know.'

'And I'll never break another promise either.'

'Yeah,' Kim said, her face breaking into a grin. 'And pigs might fly.'

23

I had never seen Todd look so serious.

'Rosie Ryan,' he said. 'You are incorrigible. First, you almost get killed by your brother-in-law. Then you commit a break and enter of someone's property. And then, to really cap things off, you come close to getting killed by a psychopath.'

We were sitting in the front window of Sandy's Diner. It was early, and the day was bright, and the ocean calm and quiet. It was a welcome reprieve after the events of the previous night. Karen Vickery had been arrested for multiple homicides. The police had matched the note sent to me with the paper at her home. More importantly, a request had been put through to Coopertell police in Western Australia asking for dental records that would prove her true identity.

'I can't say that life isn't interesting,' I said weakly.

'Your idea of interesting is obviously different to mine.'

He took a sip of his coffee as a familiar figure passed by the diner. Excusing myself, I headed outside and caught up with him.

'Keith,' I said. 'What are you up to?'

'Leaving town.'

'Really? Your work here is done? No more demolitions? No more vigilantism?'

A smile creased Keith's lips. 'I'm sure I don't know what you're talking about.'

'Yeah. Whatever. Anyway...' I wasn't sure how to continue. It was hard to know what to say to someone you both liked and disliked. 'Thanks. I mean it.'

'You're welcome.' Keith paused. 'I had a nice time at that barbeque. In fact, I haven't laughed that much in years. In my line of business, there's not a lot of laughing.'

'You could always change businesses.'

'That's easier said than done,' he sighed and shook his head. 'You remember charades? Trampoline?'

I smiled. 'Party pooper?'

Giving me a final nod, Keith headed off down the street. I watched him till he was out of sight before returning to Sandy's.

'Keith's leaving town?' Todd said.

'Yep. He's off.'

'So he's finished?'

I thought about the boatshed. 'Yes,' I said. 'He's done.'

Kim came jogging down the footpath, saw us, and waved.

Motioning her over, I gave Kim an enormous hug. She was sticky from her run, but I didn't care.

'Here she is,' Todd said as Kim squeezed in beside me. 'The hero of the hour.'

I nodded. 'How lucky am I to have a friend like her?'

'I'm lucky too,' Kim told Todd. 'Though I've got a few questions that still need answering.'

'Like what?'

'Well, that hole in the floor at Jean and Robert's place for starters.'

'Ah.' That had baffled me too. 'This is only a guess,' I said, 'but you recall that Jean and Robert said they'd never move from their home?'

'Yes. They seemed quite vehement about it.'

'I suspect that Jamie's ashes have been buried under the house.'

'I see,' Kim said. 'That makes sense. What do you think will happen with Ray and Robyn Pennington? And Philip and Robyn?'

'I don't know if anything will change.'

'Ray said that Philip was involved with Cynthia. Was that just sour grapes?'

I chuckled. 'Cynthia did visit Philip quite a bit,' I said. 'Although she was an older woman and certainly not his lover, as Ray theorised. I should have realised it when I met Philip. I had a vague feeling that I knew him from somewhere. It wasn't that I knew him. It was that I'd just met Georgie.'

'You mean...'

'Philip and Georgie are brother and sister, and Cynthia was their mother. She was never around when they were growing up. In fact, she virtually abandoned them. Later in life, she wanted to mend broken bridges. She was able to re-establish contact with Georgie, but forming a relationship with her son wasn't so easy. He'd moved to Port Logan, not realising his mother already lived there.'

'How did you work all this out?' Todd asked.

'I didn't—at first. Georgie told me her brother lived in Queensland. It was a lie. Only this morning did I remember that Georgie's name was really Georgiana, and the boat's name was *Great Expectations*. Lovely name for a boat, but of course, it comes from the Dicken's novel. In that book, the older sister is named Georgiana, and the brother's name is—'

'Philip,' Kim finished. 'I should have realised.'

'People don't read the classics anymore,' I said. 'Our loss.'

Todd smiled. 'So all the mysteries of Port Logan are finally solved.'

'Well...' I hesitated.

'What is it?'

I didn't speak for a moment—and then I told them.

After Kim saved my life, we'd returned to Monica and Nola's

place. Of course, after almost dying twice in twenty-four hours, I'd been unable to sleep. I'd gotten up and taken a walk to Piper beach. The storm had passed by then, and the ocean was flat and calm. The moon cast its reflected glow upon it like diamonds on a velvet sheet.

And that's when I saw it. A dark shape broke the surface about a hundred metres offshore. For two or three seconds it lingered there. Then it had slid beneath the waves, leaving the ocean calm as if it had never been there at all.

Kim and Todd gaped at me.

'So you saw it,' Kim said. 'You saw the monster.'

'I saw something,' I said. 'I don't know what.'

'It could have been a whale,' Todd said. 'Or a seal.'

'Maybe.'

'You know me. I need—'

'Evidence.'

Kim sighed. 'You two are hopeless,' she said. 'You'll get eaten by the monster one night in your beds—and then you'll know!'

'Until then,' Todd said, 'the only kind of monster I'll believe in is the human kind. Thanks to both of you, Karen Vickery is now safely behind bars and probably will be for life.'

'Well,' I said. 'At least things can finally get back to normal.'

Kim raised an eyebrow.

'Almost normal,' I grumbled, turning to Todd. 'I've

promised Kim that I'm going to do more exercise. Maybe even lose some weight.'

Todd looked me up and down. 'I think you're perfect as you are.'

'Really?' My eyes met his. 'Thanks.'

'Perfect,' he said, 'apart from your foolhardy nature, the way you leap without looking, and the constant law breaking.'

'And your height,' Kim added. 'You're *way* too tall. And you always complain about my movies whenever we have films nights, Rosie. Like there's something wrong with flesh-eating zombies. Oh, and you're pig-headed. It's like talking to a brick wall sometimes.'

'Okay.' I glared at them. 'Anything else? Any other grievous faults that you find so hard to take?'

'Give us time,' Kim said.

'Yeah.' Todd took my hand and smiled. 'We'll think of something.'

But the adventure doesn't end here!

Catch Rosie's next mystery in:

Flowers, Fish and Murder!

ABOUT THE AUTHOR

Darrell Pitt is a prolific author, with more than two dozen novels in print. Writing for both young and old alike, Darrell's books traverse multiple genres including cozy mysteries, science-fiction and adventure stories. A proud resident of Melbourne, Australia, Darrell shares his home with his wife and says he owns too many books (as if such a thing were possible!)

His literary journey began with a passion for crafting short stories in his youth, eventually evolving into full-length novels. Among his accolades, "A Toaster on Mars" earned a prestigious spot on the shortlist for the 2017 Russell Prize, showcasing Darrell's unique brand of humour. His novel, "The Firebird Mystery", received commendation from The Children's Book Council of Australia as a Notable book in 2015.

Darrell's Teen Superhero series has garnered widespread acclaim, while his Rosie Ryan books are a series of delightful mysteries set in a distinctly Australian environment. Among the books he's currently working on are a tech-thriller, a time-travel novel, and a mystery book set in 1960's Victoria.